GOLD BADGES

&

DARK SOULS

A Larry Gillam and Sam Lovett Novel

by

William N. Gilmore

William N. Gilmore

First Printing

Book cover design by William N. Gilmore and by Arewa Lanre of graphics_pro360 (a fiverr.com seller)

This is a work of fiction. Names, characters, places, organizations, and incidents are the product of the author's imagination or are used fictitiously, and any resemblance to actual persons, living or dead, businesses, companies, events, or locals are entirely coincidental.

ISBN: 978-1-946689-00-9

Manufactured by CreateSpace

www.createspace.com

Printed in the United States of America

GOLD BADGES

&

DARK SOULS

To MELINDA,
THANK you FoR youR
SoppoRT

William N. Gilmore
ApD

William N. Gilmore

Acknowledgements

To my wife, Esther, our family and friends, for encouragement, ideas, understanding, and love.

To Deanna Oaks (and her red pen), Bryan Powell, the late Dana Freeman, and the rest of the Paulding County (GA) Writers' Guild for all of their help.

pcwg-ga@pcwgga.org

To all the men and women in uniform, our veterans, our wounded warriors, and those who gave their lives, so all of us could live ours in this wonderful country, a constitutional republic, free and safe.

Thank You.

Part of my family's military service:

Grandfather: John D. Warner, PVT, U. S. Army, WWII (deceased)

Father: William N. Warner; Sp5, U. S. Army (Korea) (deceased)

Step-father: Robert B. Gilmore; CAPT., U. S. Army; Ret. At Schofield Barracks, Pearl Harbor, HI., December 7, 1941 (deceased)

Brother: Larry J. Pankau; LTC., U. S. Air Force; Ret. B-52 pilot, Viet Nam vet. (6 tours), Awarded the DFC (deceased)

Brother: Allan John Pankau; SR, U. S. Navy (deceased)

Brother-in-law: J. C. Williams Jr.; A/1C, U. S. Air Force

Niece: Cindy Pankau Carmack; PO/1C, U. S. Navy; Ret.

Nephew: Chris Pankau; PFC, U. S. Army

Myself: William N. Gilmore; SGT., U. S. Army (Germany) Viet Nam era, Military Police, Good Conduct Medal (2)

This is Book Two

of my Detective Series featuring fictional Atlanta Police Detectives Larry Gillam and Sam Lovett.

I hope you enjoyed Book One

"Blue Bloods & Black Hearts"

Book Three, "Blue Knights & White Lies" will be coming out later this year.

These are works of fiction; however, I did incorporate some aspects of my twenty-seven years on the Atlanta Police Department and my seven years as a Military Policeman in the U.S. Army, working with various units and agencies.

I write in my own style and there may be some things which you find different from other writers; possibly even different from what is taught, or used in the course of proper novel writing.

Good. I'm different from other writers.

Please forgive any mistakes you may find.

Please let me know what you think.

This is for your entertainment.

Enjoy.

Books by

William N. Gilmore

Books in the Larry Gillam and Sam Lovett Series

Book One:

BLUE BLOODS

&

BLACK HEARTS

Other Books:

Saints, Sinners, Lovers and Others

Poems and Prose

From Thoughts That Arose

William N. Gilmore

CHAPTER 1

Sam Granger was not alone in his office and he didn't even know. Customers were not allowed on the impound lot at this time of night, and all the wrecker drivers had gone home or were out on assignments. The figure stood over Granger, almost laughing at the situation. *This is too easy*, he thought, and then he did laugh.

One empty bottle of booze was on the floor, another was on the desk, and Granger was clutching a third. He was lying on a couch; a hideous, green thing, which looked like it hadn't been cleaned in many, many years.

Granger was lying on his right side snoring, drool coming from his open mouth, dripping onto the ugly couch. The dark figure looked around and saw items he could use. He smiled as he constructed a plan.

He took one of the cushions from the foot of the couch and nudged Granger a couple times until he turned over on his back. He slapped Granger in the face. Granger dropped the bottle, barely moving. He slapped him again. This time, Granger put his hands up around his face. The man slapped them away.

"Wake up you drunk, come on, wake up."

Granger spoke incoherent words, but kept swatting at whatever might have stung him.

"Where's Thompson?"

"Whaa …, who are you?" Granger said, his eyes barely opening; just now aware someone was there.

He was slapped again.

Granger's eyes opened more this time. "What do you want?"

"Tell me where Thompson is."

"He's dead. Who are you? Stop hitting me," Granger pleaded.

"Tell me about Thompson and I will. How did he die?"

"I think he drowned. The fat bastard couldn't swim. Who are you? What do you want?"

"When did you last hear from him?"

"I don't know."

The man raised his hand and Granger begged, "Don't hit me no more, mister. I don't remember."

The man hit him anyway. "You better remember. Now tell me, when did you last see Thompson? Think!"

Granger started crying. "He went out on a call and brought one back, but I didn't see him when he returned. He got a late call, went out and he never came back. We found out later it was a bogus call. He was set up. Somebody got him and drove the wrecker in the river, or he drove it in, and he can't swim. I think he drowned. He can't swim," Granger slurred, falling back into a stupor.

The man grabbed him and shook him. "Does he have any family around here?"

"His mother's in a home. We are his family here. He was my best friend."

"So, he would call or contact *you,* if anyone?"

"Yes. Leave me alone. Bubba's dead. Can't you see that?"

"The man raised his hand again. "And you haven't seen him or heard from him?"

"No. He's dead I told you."

He hit Granger in the stomach, not hard, but enough to cause him to react by sitting up and gasping. The intruder took a large slice of a cold, leftover pizza sitting in a box on a table, stuffing it in Granger's open mouth. He put the soft fabric cushion over Granger's face, pushing him into the couch. It delivered the desired effect.

Granger, in his inebriated state, threw up, but the mixture of too much alcohol and pizza had nowhere to go. The man held down the cushion making sure the vomit stayed in Granger's mouth and windpipe.

Even as drunk as Granger was, he fought to get the man off him, but to no avail. The man outweighed him with muscle, not fat, and he wasn't drunk. Granger had been drinking all day, and it took a toll on his strength and his ability to counter the assailant. It wasn't long before Granger succumbed to the deadly assault. Shortly after Granger stopped moving, the man removed the pillow.

The man arranged Granger on the couch with the puke soaked cushion under his head. As far as he was concerned, Thompson, the wrecker driver, died with no connection to the operation. And as far as anyone would know, Granger strangled on his own puke from a combination of bad pizza and cheap whiskey.

He wiped his hands on Granger's shirt and pulled out his cell phone, calling the special number he knew by heart.

The general kept late hours, so it was not uncommon for him to receive calls during this time. When the call was transferred to him, he answered only, "Yes?"

"Good evening sir, I just wanted to inform you that I've confirmed the wrecker driver is not an issue. His supervisor at the impound lot suffered an unfortunate fatal accident this evening involving his eating and drinking habits. It seems he choked to death while he was intoxicated."

"What a shame. Enjoy your weekend, captain."

"Thank you, sir. Any chance you've changed your mind about the game?"

"No. However, thank you, again. I will see you Monday morning."

The captain left the impound office. There was still no one around to see him leave and make the short trek to his vehicle. He got in and made another call.

"Lieutenant, there's been a terrible accident over at the impound yard. I want this handled like the bum on Griffin Street. No investigation needed. It was an accidental death by choking. Is that clear?"

Lieutenant Jones acknowledged the information and asked, "What about this body?"

"It was an accident, lieutenant. He's going to the morgue and he might get an autopsy, but it's a pretty good bet that even if they do, nothing will be found."

"Alright, I've got someone who can sweep it under the rug, and get the right report written to make it quick and painless. No questions asked."

"Are you going to handle this yourself?"

"No, it's not good for me to be seen at too many incidents which don't involve drugs. Plus, it's my night off."

"So, you're telling me you have this covered?"

"I have it covered."

Getting the response he required, the captain put his phone away and drove off.

He was looking forward to a day or so away. He didn't have a girlfriend. At least, no one in the area, and he didn't want to go to the game alone. There was no one at The Facility he wanted to ask. He thought about Jenny for a split second, but she was restricted to The Facility and it would be a major break of protocol to take her out into the public. Too bad, she was cute.

13

He got an idea and hoped it wasn't too late to call. He got his phone out again as he drove through the main gate of Fort McPherson, returning the salute of the Military Policeman standing there waving him through. As he drove over to the BOQ, he made the connection and the party answered.

"Morris."

"Morris, this is King. What's the situation?"

"Everything's quiet right now. Our pigeon is home watching porno movies and getting drunk. He's alone. He received a call and made a few more. That's all. Any orders?"

"No. I just wanted to check in. You know you're being reassigned on Monday?"

"Yes. I got the word this afternoon. Any other time I might have been sorry to go, but I can see this dork is going to be a real pain."

"As I told the general, he's an idiot, but he's our idiot, and he's already caused us to have to cover our butts more than once. He knew it wasn't your fault, being compromised, and that's why you're only being reassigned and not decommissioned. He knows you're one of our best."

"It worried me there for a bit. I signed on for this and I know my duty, but I'll tell you right now, if Jones is to be taken out, I volunteer for the job. Hell, I'd pay to do it."

"You might just get your chance at that. Listen, the other reason I called was since there's no activity scheduled for the weekend and the relief team will be on, I got hold of some tickets for the Brave's game on Sunday. Want to go?"

"Yeah, that sounds good. I was hoping to catch a game or two while I was here, but with all this crap going on, I didn't see any chance of that happening. Thanks."

"I'll call you tomorrow and we can set it up. Just make sure he stays put and doesn't get into any more trouble, or rather, get *us* in any more trouble."

"I don't think you have to worry about that too much. He has a whole sack full of videos and a fridge full of beer to go through. If that doesn't work, I have a new choke hold I've been practicing I can try on him."

"I'm sure you do. Just remember, he may still be valuable to some degree. Let's not waste our resources."

"I ordinarily wouldn't waste my time, but it would be so much fun."

"Okay," the captain laughed. "I'll talk to you tomorrow."

William N. Gilmore

CHAPTER 2

Everyone sat staring at Bubba Thompson. No one spoke a word. No one moved. It was as if he were a bomb and any little thing could set him off. No one dared to even breathe for a moment.

All three with open mouths, no words escaping; their hearts pounding loud enough to drown out their thoughts; eyes bulged in shock, threatening to pop out; a cartoon drawing if there ever was one, but not the funny kind. Maybe one from a horror comic book; one which would give kids nightmares.

Finally, Gillam spoke. Very slow and deliberate, he asked, "You saw Lieutenant Jones kill Doctor Kim?"

"Yeah, that's what I've been saying. And I thought that you and your partner, or partners," Bubba said, looking at Debbie, "were in on it. Doris didn't think so, but I couldn't be sure. I knew I wouldn't be able to hide forever, so I thought if I got one of you to confess, I could get you all arrested and be safe that way."

"You said Jones has two guys working for him, is this one of them?" Gillam said, pulling a folded piece of paper from a pocket and passing it over to Thompson.

"Yeah, that's one of them. Is he a cop too?" Bubba asked, handing the paper back.

"We don't know who he is," Gillam said, handing the paper to Debbie. Sam already saw him in person.

The paper showed a photocopy of Gillam's identification, only with the picture of the man posing as the property clerk instead of Gillam. It was the one copied at the crime lab while being used by the imposter.

Sam looked over at Gillam, "Okay, now what?"

"First, I take some aspirin. Then we go over to the impound lot, confront Granger, and see what he knows about Jones. Then we find that son of a bitch, beat the crap out of him; within an inch of his life if we have to, and find out what the hell is going on."

"I'm going too," Bubba said, quickly.

"Oh, no. You're staying right here. Everyone thinks you're dead and dead you will be for real if you go out there," Gillam said, pointing towards the door. "You're a witness and I'm not letting anything happen to you. You might be my one chance to nail that bastard."

"What about Doris?" The big man asked.

"Doris is safe," Gillam said. "No one knows that she saw anything as long as you stay here and she keeps her mouth shut."

"Okay, but I meant she's parked around the corner waiting on me."

"Oh, now that's just great," Gillam exclaimed. "What is she driving?"

"She's in a red Neon."

"Then we'll stop and tell her to go home."

"She'll think you killed me?"

"Call her and tell her to go home, yourself then."

"She'll think you got a gun to my head or something."

"For God's sake, man," Gillam said, his frustration coming out, "call her and tell her to come to the apartment and she can see for herself. Don't make this any harder than it already is. She can stay here with you while we're gone to the impound yard to see if Granger is still there. He may even still be passed out. It shouldn't take more than an hour or so."

Bubba called Doris and she reluctantly drove to the apartment. She refused to get out of her car until she saw Bubba come outside, come over to her car, and tell her in person it was all right.

"What is going on?" she asked, trying to look around Bubba.

"They want to talk to Sam about that lieutenant that came to his office. The one that killed the guy in the meat wagon."

"See, I told you they weren't part of it," admonishing Bubba as she got out of the car.

They quickly walked to Gillam's apartment. When they got in, Bubba introduced Doris. She shook hands with everyone but Gillam who was still sitting on the couch holding the cloth to his head. She looked up at Bubba and he shrugged.

"Oops," he said, holding his head down.

"Don't I know you from somewhere?" Gillam asked her.

19

"You may know my voice better; I'm one of the senior police dispatchers."

"Of course," said Lovett, "you used to date Simmons."

She turned her head and gave Sam a look which if it could kill, he would already be buried and nothing but dust. Sam quickly changed the subject.

"If we're going over to the impound lot, we should go before it gets too late. I still have a dinner waiting for me at home."

"We're going to the impound lot?" Doris asked.

"Not you and Bubba. You're staying here, at least, till we get back. We can't take a chance of Bubba being seen if people think he's dead. What you saw out at Armour Drive is the only real connection we have between Lieutenant Jones and Doctor Kim's death. I need for you both to stay here."

"May I talk with you, Detective Gillam, in private if you don't mind?" She looked over at Bubba and he had a quizzical look. "It's okay, I'll be right back."

Doris and Gillam stepped outside, away from everyone's questioning eyes and out of earshot.

"Detective, I need to tell you something."

"I already know about you and Granger. I'm sure it's a little strange being here with Bubba and all."

"Well, yes, you're right about that, but I think I need to go with you to the lot."

"And why is that?"

"I might be able to help you there. If he's not there, I know where certain files and documents are. You see, Sam doesn't trust anyone. And if he *is* there, then I might be able to convince him to give you those files. Sam's a great guy, but he does a little business, ah …, under the table. He gets things or does things for people. I know he's done business with Lieutenant Jones in the past. I'm not sure exactly what, and I never get involved in Sam's business, but I don't trust the lieutenant. And with all this going on, I want to make sure Bubba is safe too."

"Granger thinks he is your boyfriend, is that right?"

"Sam likes to think he's my boyfriend, and we do date some, but he's not my only boyfriend. I like going out with a lot of guys. A girls got needs, you know."

"He doesn't know everything about you and Bubba?"

"Bubba might work for him, but they're the best of friends. I don't want to hurt anybody."

"So, right now, you're seeing both of them, and neither of them knows what it's all about, and it's best if it stays that way."

"That's right," she smiled. "I'm glad you understand. I need to be careful about what I say or do in front of them when they're together. I'm also afraid that Sam might have gotten into something he can't handle and he'll get Bubba involved. He's sweet, a little slow sometimes, and he doesn't need to be getting mixed up with any of that."

Larry rubbed his head. "I think Bubba has already

become involved with whatever Sam is into. I'll tell you what we'll do. You'll go with us to the lot, just in case, but you'll stay in the car until, and if we need you."

"That's a deal."

"But Bubba stays here, out of sight. There will be no mention of him at all. He's dead, remember? That's the best way to keep him safe."

"Okay. When do we leave?"

"Now."

They went back into the apartment. "Sam," Gillam started. "You're going with me and Doris. Debbie, you take your car and go home. Bubba, you stay here, out of my fridge, don't open the door, and no phone calls."

All of them protested at once. There was mass confusion at first until Larry shouted out.

"Enough!" He grabbed his head as it throbbed once more. "This is the way it's going to be, and there will be no more discussion about it. I know what I'm doing and I have this worked out. Bubba has to stay here because everyone thinks he's dead; we want them to keep thinking that. He can't be seen anywhere. Debbie, sweetheart, I love you dearly, but this is not your job, and I can't have you, as a civilian, backing us up right now. I need you at home so Sam and I won't worry about you, and as someone I can contact if things go south. Doris is going with us to the impound lot in case she can be of any help with things there, but she won't be put in any danger."

Debbie spoke out. "All right. I'll go home, but you've got to let me know what's going on. And you're already so far south, you can shake hands with penguins."

"That's good. I'll have to remember that one," Gillam smiled.

"And keep dinner warm for me," Sam reminded her.

"You might find the couch made up for you, old man."

"What'd I do?" Sam asked, holding up his hands.

Larry, Sam, Debbie, and Doris headed out the door.

"Lock this door behind us and don't open it for anyone," Gillam told Thompson. "I don't care if they say they're the Chief of Police or even the President."

"What would the President be doing at *your* door?"

"Collecting taxes and taking away my guns."

The door slammed and Larry heard the lock engage. He wished there were others for his refrigerator and his cabinets.

"Why would Sam worry about *her*?" Doris asked.

William N. Gilmore

CHAPTER 3

Gillam drove as Lovett explained to Doris about the two Sam's. The drive only took about twenty minutes, but as they got near the entrance, they could see there was a flurry of activity around the lot. There were police cars, a fire truck, a rescue unit, and an ambulance. Doris sat up from her seat in the back, trying to see better. Trying to see the other Sam.

"This doesn't look good," Lovett said, forgetting for a moment about Doris.

"No, and I don't want to make it worse by going in there just yet. Sam, do you see anyone in there you know?"

"Not yet," Sam answered. "There are too many lights going around for me to see anyone clearly. I mainly want to make sure who's not there."

"Yeah, I know what you mean. He could be anywhere."

Gillam parked his car on a side street. "You two stay here. I'm going to see if I can find out what's going on."

Gillam left the two in the car and walked over to the entrance gate where a patrol officer was positioned.

"Howdy. What's going on here?" Gillam inquired.

"I'm sorry, sir, you can't enter right now. There's nothing to see."

Gillam didn't recognize the officer and believed it would

be all right to pursue the questioning for more information.

"Did somebody get hurt in there?"

The officer wasn't about to give up any information. "Sir, I'm going to have to ask you to step back. Go on home. There's nothing to see here."

Gillam could see this was no rookie and he wasn't going to get anywhere this way. He pulled his ID and badge out.

"Sergeant Gillam," he said, giving his rank this time, but not his division. "I was just driving by and wanted to see if I could be of any help."

"Oh, sorry, sergeant, I didn't recognize you. Nothing much to worry about. One of the workers here seems to have choked to death. They just got him in the ambulance and are about to take off. He was DOA of the first unit."

"Did anyone say who it was?

"I think they said his name was Gardner or Grazier. Something like that."

"Could it have been Granger?"

"Yeah, that's it. Did you know him, sergeant?"

"Not really. Just as someone who ran the yard. Was there anyone with him?"

"I don't think so. The first unit on the scene found the front gate open with the lock on the chain open and the guy in the office alone. Said the guy was lying on a couch and choked on his own vomit of what looked like whiskey and pizza. Not a pretty sight, or smell, I'm sure."

"Well, who made the call on him then?"

"I don't know. That's a good question. Now I see why you're the sergeant and I'm still only an officer."

"Who's in charge here?"

"That would have been my shift supervisor, Sergeant Conner. He checked it out and saw it was an accidental death, made sure we were handling it right, the proper paperwork was being filled out, stuff like that. Then he left. Do you want me to radio him?"

"No. I was just curious who was running the show. Is there anything else going on tonight?"

"It's quiet out there for a change. There's only this accidental death report being made by the responding officer. There's nothing else to do except patrol. Beats getting shot at I guess," he laughed.

The fire truck and rescue unit exited the yard with the ambulance right behind. The flashing lights had been turned off. There was no need for them now, especially the ambulance. All the officers went to their cars and were leaving as well. Several, not even dispatched there, just wanted to see the body; it was that slow.

"Well, I guess the circus is over for now. You have a good night, sergeant. Thanks for stopping." The officer waited for the last patrol car to exit and closed the gate behind him, closing the open lock to secure it. He got into the passenger side of the patrol car and left with all the others, leaving Gillam standing there at the secured gate.

Gillam walked back over to his car. He wasn't sure what he was going to tell Doris. No need to lie to her. He got back in the car.

"It was Sam, wasn't it?" she asked, right away. Already knowing.

"Yes."

"Is he …, is he dead?"

"I'm afraid so."

Doris began to cry, but only a little. "I knew it would end up like this. I warned him it would all catch up. Was he shot?"

"No."

"Was he stabbed?"

"No. The officer told me he choked to death. Apparently, he was eating and drinking and he just choked. It's sad, but it appears it was an accident."

Doris almost laughed through her tears. "Choked? Well, I always knew he would die doing something he enjoyed. Either in bed, at the poker table, or with a fork in his hand."

"Well he didn't need a fork this time. He choked on whiskey and pizza."

"What did you say?" Doris questioned, her crying stopping, staring straight at Gillam.

"The officer said that he choked on whiskey and pizza. Apparently, while he was passed out drunk, lying on a couch, he threw up, couldn't breathe, and strangled."

"Detective, Sam never ate a pizza in his life. He couldn't. He can't eat cheese, tomatoes, onions, peppers, mushrooms, or seafood. After I got off, I picked up an anchovy pizza for myself and a plain, ham sub for him. I came over to the yard to spend some time with him because he felt so bad about Bubba. I couldn't tell him Bubba was alive. Not yet. Now, he'll never know," she said, the tears now returning.

"He was drinking," she continued. "A lot. He didn't want to eat. He fell asleep, and I was running late to meet with Bubba, and left the pizza behind. There is no way he would have touched it. He didn't put that pizza in his mouth, someone else did."

William N. Gilmore

CHAPTER 4

"We need to get in there and check the scene," Gillam said. "I don't want to tip off the owner or anyone else. Sam, help me over this fence."

"I can't lift your fat butt up that high. And besides, you'll get yourself caught on that razor wire at the top for sure."

"Wouldn't it be better to open the gate with a key?" Doris said, as she stood there with one hand on her hip and swinging a key ring with several keys around a finger on the other. "For those late-night rendezvous."

"Why didn't you tell us you had a key to the gate? Gillam asked, a bit frustrated.

"You didn't ask," Doris gave the classic answer. "See, I knew you would need my help."

"I think you held back a little of the truth about your relationship with Granger. Sam, go get my car," Gillam said, throwing him his own keys. "We'll unlock the gate and lock it back after you drive in."

Sam took off at a trot and returned driving Gillam's car. He turned off the lights before going through the open gate and waited for them while they secured it back. Gillam and Doris got in and Sam drove over to the main office building.

"I was afraid you wouldn't be able to reach the peddles,"

Gillam laughed.

"I've got blocks tied to my feet, Sam returned."

They pulled into a parking space, exited the car, and went to the main office complex. The door was locked, but again, Doris had a key for that as well, smiling at them as she unlocked it.

They told her to wait while they made sure no one was left in the building. It took about ten minutes and then they called her in after it was cleared. It was possible someone had been missed, but not likely. It was best to be safe.

Granger's office was in the back with a window facing the vehicle storage area. Not much of a view, but it provided a bit of privacy.

Doris was a little on edge about going into the office, even though it was one she visited many times before. Gillam noticed her hesitation.

"You can wait out there if you want. Sam and I can handle this part alone."

"No, I want to. It may be the last time I ever go in there, but maybe I can do some good now. Maybe I can feel Sam's presence one more time."

She opened the unlocked door to his office and they all went in. There were items scattered on the floor that indicated the rescue team attempted to resuscitate Granger. Something they usually tried no matter what the condition of the person. Sometimes it was a true attempt and sometimes it was a show for the family, or for insurance, or so they didn't get sued for not trying.

The couch in the office must have been where Granger was lying. There was a pillow with stains and a foul odor on the floor. A pizza box was on a table next to the couch. Lovett went over and opened the pizza box and there was one slice of an anchovy pizza remaining.

"This the pizza you were talking about?" he asked Doris, picking up the box and showing it to her.

"Yes, that's it. There were three slices still in the box when I left. I ate the other three. I know Sam wouldn't have touched it. Maybe one of the fireman or police officers ate it."

"I don't think so," Lovett said, shaking his head. "It's not something you want to do at a site where someone just died after eating something. You don't try the food."

"I don't think he did either," Gillam said, looking in a small refrigerator in the corner by the table. Pointing into the fridge, "That's the sandwich you brought him, right?"

Doris nodded.

"If he was that hungry," Sam surmised, "he would have eaten the ham sandwich before the pizza, but I guess he was more interested in drinking. There are several empty whiskey bottles lying around. He was getting pretty snookered when we came by earlier. I guess that was before you got here. I would say he had been drinking the whole day with very little food, if any."

33

Gillam got on his cell phone and hit the button for the new speed dial number he put in. The receiving end rang several times before it was answered.

"Fulton County Medical Examiner's Office, may I help you?

"Who's this?" Gillam asked not recognizing the voice.

"This is Doctor Michaels. I'm the new Assistant Chief Medical Examiner. Who is calling, may I ask?"

"This is Detective Gillam, is Doctor Higdon available?"

"I'm sorry, detective, the doctor is sleeping now. He told me to tell you if you called that he has some information for you about the items you gave him and he'll talk with you more in the morning. I'm not real sure what's going on, but he and Jaccob are spending the night here. I came in for my usual shift and the next thing I know I'm taking Doctor Kim's place. I didn't want it this way. It was a tragedy."

"Yes, we all feel that way. He'll be missed. I'm sure that if Doctor Higdon picked you to take Doctor Kim's place, he has the utmost confidence in you."

"Thank you, detective. Was there anything else I can do for you?"

"Yes, there is. There's a body by the name of Sam Granger that may be there by now. He is listed as an accidental death, asphyxiation. I need a complete work-up on him. Including stomach contents and any abnormal items such as bruising, skin punctures, anything that would show something other than accidental death, if you catch my drift."

"Yes, he was just delivered about five minutes ago. He'll be put on the waiting list for examination. Are you trying to tell me it may be a homicide?"

"If you can't do it, would you please tell Doctor Higdon when he gets up?"

"Now I didn't say I couldn't do it. I just want to know if there are things I should be aware of to help me with my examination."

"He was very drunk and he may have had some anchovy pizza stuffed in his mouth by someone else. I want to see if his stomach contained any pizza, or if there may have been any bruising from a struggle or assault."

"Thank you. That was specific enough to start. Give me a little time and I'm sure I can come up with some information for you soon."

"I'm glad we see eye to eye on this."

Gillam hung up. "Okay, let's see if that's going to lead anywhere. Doris, you said something about some files that Granger may have hidden and you were going to get them for us."

"Yeah. I don't guess Sam will need them anymore." She went over to the wall across from the desk and removed a panel. Behind the panel was a hidden space big enough to keep a few items. She reached inside and removed a folder and a large envelope. She handed the folder to Gillam. She found the envelope to contain cash; a lot of cash. "I guess Sam won't need this anymore either. He has no one else." She started to hand it to him as well.

"I don't know what you're talking about," Larry said, with a smile. "Is there anything else which we may need from the office?"

"There's nothing else here that I know about," Doris said.

"Then let's get out of here. Bubba may have eaten my cat by now."

They left the office, locking it behind them, doing the same with the building and the gate when they left the yard. This time they made sure nothing was following them. Sam even checked the sky again for black helicopters, or the slim chance of a UFO.

Gillam drove back to his apartment hoping Bubba hadn't left, and then again, to some degree, that he had. Mainly he hoped he didn't find him dead on the floor with a puddle of blood on his carpet. It would be so hard to clean up.

When they got to the apartment, there were no police cars, fire trucks, or ambulances. Gillam gave a little sigh of relief. Now to see the bad news inside.

Gillam unlocked his front door and when he opened it he peered inside first to see if everything was all right. He almost got another brain bashing from Bubba.

Bubba was standing by the entrance with the retrieved tire iron raised above his head, ready to strike.

"What are you trying to do, make sure I'm dead this time?"

"I'm so sorry, detective. I didn't know who it was. I've been so scared since you've been gone. I've sat right here watching that door, afraid someone was going to bust in and get me." Sam and Doris came in behind Larry.

Gillam's television was on and there were several food wrappers lying around as well as an unfinished bowl of cereal.

Gillam looked at Bubba. "Yeah, right. Sat right there the whole time, scared to move, huh. Well, I might have been born at night, but it wasn't last night. Is there anything left?"

"I was hungry. You left me here alone and told me I couldn't leave. I didn't know when you would come back, if ever."

"Have you seen my cat?"

"I think he ran and hid in the bedroom."

"He's a she. And she's a good judge of character."

"Did you see Sam?"

Doris and Gillam looked at each other for a long time. Her eyes began to water up again.

"Why don't you have a seat, Bubba," Gillam said as sympathetically as possible.

After the big man labored into the couch, Doris sat beside him, placing her hand on his large thigh.

"Bubba, I hate to tell you this," Doris began, barely looking him in the eyes, her voice cracking. "Sam's dead. He choked to death. It seems it was an accident." She turned and winked at Gillam and Lovett. She didn't want to tell him the truth yet. He might go out and try something drastic.

"He had been drinking too much and ate something, and he just choked. I'm sorry. I know how close the two of you were."

After Bubba's mouth dropped open, he just stared at her. He didn't say a thing. Tears started to well up in his eyes. He lowered his head, shaking it, and said, "What's next? Hasn't this day just sucked enough already? Now what?"

"It's time for us to figure out just what to do next," Lovett said.

"We have to find you a safe place to hide Bubba."

"I can't take him home with me. There's no room. I've got family coming to visit." Sam lied. "Why not let him stay here? No one knows he's here now."

"Well, what about Doris here, she could take him. Aren't they a couple now?" Gillam inquired, looking at Doris with pleading eyes.

"I have a female roommate and that would go over like a lead balloon. Scratch that idea," she said quickly, giving Gillam the evil eye.

"Looks like you win by default, Larry," Sam said, with a grin, getting Gillam back for making him climb into the Medical Examiner's wagon. "Now all you have to do is figure out which side of the bed he sleeps on."

"You're not very funny. All right, the other bedroom is an office, so you sleep on the couch" he said, looking at Bubba. And you stay away from my food. And my cat."

"But what do I eat? I'll starve."

"Not for at least a month or two. Don't worry, I'll do some shopping, you won't starve. And you can't go back to where you live. A trailer, right?"

"Yeah that's right. How'd you know that?"

"Lucky guess. Anyway, we'll need to get you some more clothes and other items because you sure can't use mine. You have any money? Please tell me you have some money."

Bubba held up his hands, empty palms up and shrugged his shoulders.

"That's just great. I guess I have to adopt you too."

Doris took some cash from the envelope she found at Granger's office and handed it to Gillam. "Will this take care of it?"

Gillam looked down at the stack of hundred dollar bills Doris was handing him. It was only a small portion of what was in the envelope.

"Yeah, that should do it."

"Doris, where did you get all that money?" Bubba asked, his red eyes bugging out at the wad of cash.

"I got a bonus for doing such a good job," she said with a straight face.

Gillam and Lovett looked at each other, and somehow,

kept their snickers and comments inside.

CHAPTER 5

Saturday morning Gillam woke with Cali on his chest staring at him. It was a good thing he didn't believe in the old wives' tale about cats stealing your breath. It was eight o'clock.

He started to get up and heard a noise in the kitchen. He grabbed his 9mm on the nightstand and opened his bedroom door. He worked his way down the hall to the main living area and kitchen. When he looked around the corner, Bubba was at the stove and he could finally smell the bacon which just started to sizzle.

He came around the corner and Bubba turned and said, "Good morning, sleepyhead. I've been up for a while and I thought I'd cook up some breakfast for us. I didn't see a coffee machine and I couldn't find any instant. Where do you keep it?"

Gillam, standing there in his briefs, holding a gun, didn't seem to faze Bubba at all. Cali wasn't fazed either as she followed the scent into the kitchen and sat there staring up at them, licking her whiskers.

"I almost forgot you were here," Gillam said. "I don't have any coffee. I don't drink the stuff. I'll go take a shower and be right back. Then well make a shopping list."

Gillam returned in about fifteen minutes. Clean, shaven, dressed, and frustrated. "You had to use up all the hot water, didn't you?"

"I wasn't in the shower more than fifteen to twenty minutes. You must have a small water heater," Bubba said, smiling sheepishly.

"Today, we go over some rules while you stay here. Your *short* stay here."

Bubba fixed two plates of scrambled eggs and bacon. He found the bread and toaster in the cupboard, and the cherry preserves in the fridge. The table was set for the two of them.

Gillam sat down. He hadn't made time for a home breakfast in a while. "This looks good, Bubba. Thanks."

"I figured you might like your eggs scrambled. That's how I like mine. I fixed some over-easy on toast earlier."

"You already ate once this morning?"

"Yeah, but that was almost an hour ago. I'm still hungry."

Gillam wasn't so sure Doris gave him enough money last night.

"When we get done, I'll get your sizes, then I'll go to the store and get you some stuff. I guess you need everything; toiletries, underwear, socks, pants, and shirts."

"I don't wear any underwear."

"I think I just lost my appetite," Gillam said, pushing the plate away. "Around here, you wear underwear. I don't care if you run buck naked at your trailer. Here, you *must* wear underwear. It's one of the many rules I was going to tell you. It's non-negotiable."

"Okay. I meant I sometimes don't wear underwear, if I can't find any clean enough to wear."

"Stop! Enough about your underwear. Not another word." He took his plate and walked over to Cali's food dish and scraped the rest of the uneaten eggs and bacon into the bowl. Cali went after it like a mouse. Cali liked scrambled eggs too. The bacon was an added treat which she didn't get very often.

Gillam noticed the pile of dishes in the sink and on the stove. Broken egg shells were in the sink as well. Bubba also allowed the bacon to spatter grease all over the stove top. He didn't think it would get clean unless it cleaned itself, or he did it. He could just imagine what Bubba's trailer looked like.

"Bubba, are you going to clean up the mess in the kitchen?"

"I cooked. Don't you think you should do your share?"

Gillam was wishing he still held his gun. He was sure no jury would ever convict him.

"I'm going shopping for clothes and food. If this mess isn't cleaned up by the time I get back, you won't get either. If you starve to death, I'll bury you in the courtyard in the dead of night. Now write down your sizes on this pad while I get my keys and things, and get ready to leave. If I hear one more word out of you, I'll shoot you myself."

Bubba followed the directions and wrote down what he knew. It was more of a guess. Gillam looked at the note pad and shook his head. Bubba wrote *big* for almost everything; *very big* for the rest. Using years of experience, Gillam made a mental note of what he believed Bubba might wear.

"Now, when I get back, I don't want you there by the door ready to hit me again. Is that clear?"

Bubba nodded his head.

"Just don't open the door, don't answer the phone, and no phone calls. Just like before. Okay?" Another nod from Bubba. "I'll be back in about two hours."

Gillam went to the local super store for all the things he needed. He almost felt bad about taking the money from Doris, but not after seeing some of the prices for the food and clothes. It was for her boyfriend after all. And it really wasn't even her money.

He figured Bubba was a boxer type of guy and got a large package of six. Then he thought about having to do Bubba's laundry and got him two packs. He got several triple size shirts and extra-large pants, hoping that would be enough. He got Bubba his own shaving gear, toothbrush, comb and brush set, deodorant, and several other necessities.

He then went over to the food section and got a lot of frozen food assortments, lunchmeat, bread, and he thought as a treat, he'd get him some cupcakes. He got Cali's food and cat litter and thought of only one more item.

He made sure no one paid too much attention to him buying all the extra-large sized clothing as he headed for the checkout.

While waiting in line, in his head he went over the things which occurred the past couple of days. *What else could happen?* Then a sickening feeling struck him. What if the money Doris gave him was counterfeit?

Gillam started to sweat a little and was dancing around on his feet like he needed to use the restroom really bad. He pulled out some of the bills from his pocket and began looking at them nonchalantly hoping he didn't look suspicious. If the bills were counterfeit, they were the best he'd ever seen.

The girl at the register, smacking her gum, gave him the total. He handed over several of the bills. She grabbed one of the pens used to check for counterfeit bills and drew a line across them. He held his breath as she looked up at him and smiled. She put the money in her drawer and handed him the change. He grabbed the bags, put them in the buggy, and said a little prayer of thanks as he headed for the door.

Gillam loaded his car with his purchases, again looking around to see if anyone was paying too much attention to him. When he was satisfied no one was tailing him, he headed home. He had been gone two hours just like he said. His cell phone rang and he answered, "Gillam here."

"Hey, bud, I want to know, were you on top or bottom last night?" Lovett asked, laughing.

"You get funnier to yourself every day, don't you, you little piss ant?"

"I'm sorry. How is babysitting? Any problems?"

"Nothing to speak of, except he uses all the hot water and is eating everything in sight. I'm on the way home from the store now. I got him some clothes and stuff. Are you sure you don't have any room right now?" Gillam asked, with hope.

"Sorry, Larry, but you're on your own with Baby Huey."

"What's up with you today? Enjoying the day off?"

"I wanted to confirm with you about the game tomorrow. Debbie is anxious for you to meet her friend."

"I almost forgot. It's still on, even with everything that's happening?"

"You're the one who said we should keep things looking as normal as possible. I know how hard that is for you. There's nothing normal about you."

"What time do you want to meet?"

"The games at two, so why don't you come over about eleven, we'll have some lunch and head over from here. It will give you some time to show off your wit and charm, and make that first impression which lasts a lifetime."

"Just tell me you're not wearing shorts. I'm not going out with my lily-white legs to get sun burnt and for you to make comments about. I'm going to wear some jeans and a nice shirt. Don't under dress on my account."

"But it's going to be a nice hot day. It's a day made for shorts. I bet the girls are going to wear shorts. You're such a party pooper. Do me a favor. Wear whatever you want, but bring a pair of shorts with you just in case. You won't be sorry."

"We'll see. I'm pulling up to the apartment now. I'll talk to you in the morning if I don't talk to you later today. See ya.

"Okay, chicken legs. Talk to you later.

"Chicken legs? Why I'll—,

Sam already hung up.

Gillam grabbed one of the bags from the back of his car and headed to the front door with his keys in the other hand. As he put his key in the lock, he heard voices inside. He listened for a moment to make sure it wasn't the television. He tried the door and it was not locked. He opened the door just a crack and heard Bubba's voice along with a woman's. It was Doris.

"Bubba, it's me. I hope you both are decent. He walked into the room and they were sitting on the couch. Yes, they were decent. "Doris, what are you doing here?"

"I came over to see if Bubba needed anything. I didn't think it would hurt. I thought you would be here too."

"Bubba, didn't I tell you not to open the door?"

"Yes, but it was Doris."

"How did you know it was Doris?"

"When she knocked on the door, I didn't open the door like you said," he gave a big smile. "I asked who it was first and it was Doris."

"She knocked on the door and you asked who it was. Is that right?"

"Yes. I did what you told me. I didn't open the door until

she told me it was her."

"Okay, let's say there was a knock at the door and you asked who it was and they said, 'I'm here to kill Bubba, is he here?' What would you have said then?"

"I would have said, 'No, he's not here.' Isn't that what I'm supposed to say?"

"Don't you see how ridiculous that is? You already answered both the questions by asking who was there. They would know someone was there and they would know it was you.

If someone knocks on the door, just let them keep knocking. It's like the phone. If you don't answer it, no one knows if anyone is there. They usually assume no one is home. That's what we're trying to do with you. Keep you invisible here. No one is to know you're here."

"Doris already knows I'm here."

"Doris, can you explain it to him, please. I give up. I'm going back out to get the rest of the stuff."

"Did you get some food? I'm starving."

"Big surprise there. Did you clean up the kitchen?"

"Yes, but I still think that's unfair. I cooked. You should clean."

"Life's not fair, but it beats being dead by just a little bit. My house, my rules. You have a target on your back. You want to go out there like that, there's the door," Gillam said, pointing the way out. "I'm trying to keep you alive. You think you can do a better job, you have better resources, and you have a way out of all of this? Go ahead. We can protect you, keep you safe, and get to the bottom of all of this with your cooperation. We might be able to do it without you, but I doubt it. If I didn't think it was the best for you I'd find some other way. I'll repeat it for you so you'll understand. In here, you're safe. There's the door. Once you go out there, you're on your own, and once they know you're not dead, you soon will be. Your choice. Here, or out there?"

"Okay, already. I'm sorry. I'll listen to you from now on. It won't happen again. I swear."

Gillam went out the door shaking his head. He returned with several shopping bags and tossed one of them at Bubba. "See if these fit."

Bubba went into the bathroom at the end of the hall. The one that was designated as *his* during his stay. He came out shortly wearing one of the outfits Gillam bought. It was a perfect fit.

"Looks like I still have it," Gillam said, of himself.

The rest of the day was uneventful. Doris was allowed to stay and she and Bubba watched baseball on television.

Gillam took the folder given to him by Doris and excused himself to his bedroom along with Cali. The folder was thick with large rubber bands around it. He put off opening it until he could spend some time going over it without being disturbed.

He hoped there would be something in it that would be of help in taking down Jones, based upon what Doris said.

In the folder was a small black book and numerous papers and documents. The book contained hand written pages.

Granger had written a journal. It appeared he listed dates, times, places, and people with whom he conducted business. Some of these dealings involved loan sharking and gambling. Others were payoffs and bribes to certain officials and politicians. It looked like there was a lot more too. Granger plunged his hand into quite a few ventures, but kept a low profile as an impound lot supervisor. The documents were car titles, deeds, life insurance papers, and what appeared to be a will.

Granger apparently didn't have any family to speak of. He left cars and some property to Doris, and she was named in the will as the executor. One of the deeds was for the impound lot. *He did own it after all,* Gillam thought. He left this to Bubba.

His life insurance policy was for over half a million dollars. Most of that was to go to Doris and the rest to several charities he listed. The man was loaded, or at least, he had been. Most likely from ill-gotten gains, but now, Doris was loaded. And Bubba wasn't doing so bad himself. But how was he going to claim it if he was dead?

Gillam looked through the journal and searched for Jones' name. He found it; some very interesting reading. Gillam smiled. But he needed more than a dead man's writings and a single witness to a crime which few knew anything about. A confession would be nice. Beating a confession out of him would be better. He would work on some ideas later. Right now, he decided to go in and tell the two the bad news that their tax brackets would be increasing considerably.

William N. Gilmore

CHAPTER 6

Azira was lying in bed. He thought all night about Jenny and how he might be able to help her. However, to help her, he needed to know where she was. *She* didn't even know where she was.

He needed to devise a plan to find her, get her out, and not get caught; easier said than done. He couldn't do it himself and he wasn't sure if McGill could, or would help him. He needed to get back in touch with her and get as much information as he could and work from there. Maybe his geek friends could help. It was time for another floating-head, brainstorm session.

Jenny wasn't sleeping either. She was scared. Scared she held on to too much hope. Scared that she might be discovered and sent to jail, or worse. She desperately wanted to be free from the general and his operation. She wasn't real sure what they were up to, but she was sure she didn't want to be a part of it any more.

Bubba slept like a three-hundred-and-ninety-pound baby. He was having dreams of being rich; of being his own boss; of Doris; and of course, food.

Gillam *wished* he could sleep. Not only was he being kept awake by Bubba's snoring, he thought about that murdering, bastard Jones, who kept his dirty little hands in everything. He wondered how Jones and the government were involved, and why? These were in addition to thoughts about the blind date with Debbie's friend later that morning. Unlike most of the attempts by Lovett, this was one date he was looking forward to.

Although they were only going to a ballgame, he wanted to be able to give a good impression and be able enjoy himself as well. Something he hadn't been able to do for quite a while.

He wasn't looking for a long-term relationship, or even a one night stand. He didn't want to meet someone who wanted to change him, or think that he needed saving from his past, or even from himself. He just wanted to put behind him the past couple days, maybe the past couple of years, and all the bad things going through his head. He promised himself right then that he was going to have a good time no matter what.

He reached over and rubbed his hand over Cali's fur; she purred without moving or opening her eyes. Before long, Larry was falling asleep with a smile on his face. It wasn't Cali, and it wasn't baseball on his mind; it was long red hair and green eyes.

CHAPTER 7

Larry dressed just as he promised. Casual, but no shorts. He wasn't about to show off his lily-white, freckled legs on a first date. There was already enough to scare someone off without having them put up with that. Besides, he always went out with a weapon. Especially, anywhere in downtown Atlanta. This way he could wear his ankle gun. Nowhere to hide it while wearing shorts. Not comfortably anyway.

He left Bubba on the couch watching TV. He made him promise not to open the door or make his presence known. Larry was sure his neighbors thought he was seeing someone, especially with Doris coming and going now. He was glad no one said anything in passing. It might have been hard to explain.

Larry drove to Sam's, continually wiping his hands on his trousers. Sweaty hands, increased heart rate, silly grinning. All signs he was nervous and anxious. He just hoped he didn't make a fool of himself.

He thought about bringing some flowers, but thought that might have been a bit overboard. He did take a bottle of nice wine for lunch; something which would be an icebreaker if he got tongue-tied or found nothing intelligent to say.

He pulled in the driveway, turned off his motor and took a deep breath. He wiped his hands one more time, got out, and headed for the door. Before he even got to the door, Debbie opened it, greeting him.

Giving him a big hug, she said, "How's your new roommate working out?"

"He snores like a pig with a matching apatite and manors. I'll pay you to take him off my hands. Name your price."

"Why don't you let him go over to the impound lot and stay there?"

"He's still unofficially dead. As much as I hate it, he's going to have to stay hidden just a while longer until Sam and I can figure this out. Believe me, he wants to be gone just as bad as I want him to be. It seems I'm cramping his style. His love life is suffering."

"Speaking of love life, come on in and I'll introduce you to someone."

Larry swallowed hard. He wished now he had drunk the wine before coming over.

"Here's a little something for lunch or whenever the time is right," he said, handing the bottle over to Debbie.

"Thanks, that's so thoughtful of you. I wish Sam had thought of that." Larry followed her to the back yard where Sam was sitting in a chair talking to a girl with her back to Larry. The long red hair glimmered in the sun like spun copper.

"Hey, look who decided to show up," Debbie announced.

"Hey there, old man," Sam said.

Larry never heard him. He couldn't take his eyes off the

girl as she turned and smiled. She was wearing sunglasses which she began to remove. Her eyes were in fact green; not the green of emeralds, but the green of the ocean as the sun shone on it just the right way, mesmerizing you. She took his breath away.

He did not see Sam get up, nor take his hand and begin pumping it, or what he was saying. Nothing else mattered just then. She rose from the chair and she was wearing light-blue shorts which made her legs look like they were five feet long.

Larry didn't mean to stare, but nothing right then could have torn his eyes away. He faintly heard Debbie as she was giving him a slight push with her hand on the small of his back.

"Larry, I want you to meet my friend, Connie Preston. Connie, this is Larry Gillam, Sam's partner, but more important, our good friend."

Larry took her hand in his. It felt stronger than he thought it would. He barely needed to look down to see into her eyes. "It's my pleasure to meet you, Connie," he said, hoping he could get the words out right and not sound like a blithering idiot.

"I'm glad I finally get to meet you too, Larry. I've heard a lot of good things about you from both Debbie and Sam."

Larry was about to say something cute about what they might have said, but decided just before it came out that now was not the time to start mouthing off stupid stuff. Instead he said, "I heard wonderful things about you as well, and so far, I can see everything is just as they said."

He was still holding her hand and it was getting to that

awkward point that he may have held it too long. He reluctantly
let go of her hand, releasing the grip ever so slightly until their
hands no longer touched. Already, he missed it.

She smiled, blushing slightly. "Thank you."

Debbie looked over at Sam and winked. Sam flashed a
big grin and raised his eyebrows up and down quickly several
times.

"Okay, everyone," Debbie began, "we've only got about
an hour before we have to leave for the game. It's time to eat. If
you don't like it, tough. Everything's on the table in the dining
room. If there's anything you need, just ask Sam."

"Me?" Sam said, with a look of surprise. "Why me?
You're the one who put this on. You're the hostess, the cook,
and the waitress, all in one. I'm just the food critic."

"Don't forget," Debbie added, "you're also the head
dishwasher, busboy, and garbage man, and if you're not careful,
you'll be the main guard on the dog house tonight."

"Right," Sam said, as he grabbed a towel from a chair
and put it over his arm. "Your table is ready Madam, Monsieur,"
he continued in a very bad French accent. "Right this way if you
please," bowing and ushering the way with an over exaggerated
wave of his hand and arm. We have the very finest for your
dining pleasure."

"That's enough out of you, Mr. Chevalier," Debbie said.

Both Larry and Connie laughed as they went in to the
dining room. Larry pulled out a chair for Connie and she sat,

looking up at him with a smile, thanking him. Larry melted into a chair next to her. He was feeling like a schoolboy with his first crush. He hoped it wasn't showing too much.

Debbie fixed up a nice lunch which included roasted chicken breast and rice, along with some garden vegetables. The wine Larry brought went well with the meal. Talk around the table was mainly about Larry and Connie and their jobs. Connie was a teacher in a private school. Her majors were in math and science.

"Connie, let me ask you something on a scientific matter, if you don't mind?" Sam began with a grin.

Larry knew this was going to be about him in some way.

"Sure, go ahead," she answered.

"Do you believe in UFO's?"

"Now, Sam!" Debbie exclaimed, knowing there was going to be a dig at Larry.

"No, I don't mind," Connie said. "It's a very important question these days. I can't believe we are alone in this vast universe. It only makes since that there are many other planets with life. Some may be microbes and others may be highly advanced. Advanced enough to be able to travel in or through space to our planet. What their intentions might be is anyone's guess. I just hope they're friendly."

Larry fell in love right then. He smiled and stuck his tongue out at Sam. Sam gave Larry the finger. The girls laughed.

"Beam me up Scotty, there's no intelligent life in this

house today," Sam said, pretending to talk into a hand-held communication device.

"Well, not in the chair you're sitting in anyway," Debbie said. The girls laughed again with Larry joining in this time.

After lunch, the girls shooed the boys outside while they cleaned up. Debbie knew there would be talk about their case and didn't want to bore Connie with any of that. Besides, she wanted to hear what she thought of Larry.

"Well, what do you think? Was I right, or was I right?" Debbie asked with a smile.

"He's cute all right. You have to remember it's been a while for me, so let me go slow. I still have some issues to deal with, and I agreed to be open-minded and give it a chance, and so far, I'm okay and comfortable with everything. Let's just have some fun and see how it goes. He does have a nice smile and he seems to be genuine. He's a gentleman and he's funny as well as being interesting. I like him."

"I understand your fears", Debbie said. "I'm not going to push you. Going slow is best. Sam and I dated for over two years before we got really serious and another year before we got married. Dating a cop is trying at best and being married to one is even worse. I will tell you though, if I didn't have Sam, Larry wouldn't be a bad substitute. I think he's got a cute butt too." Both girls laughed and watched as the two friends walked away from them.

Sam led Larry out to the middle of the back yard where

Stella was chained to a runner. She ran up to Larry and flipped over on her back for a belly rub. Larry didn't disappoint her. As he rubbed the big dog's stomach, Sam asked, "Well, what do you think about Connie?"

"Wow!" he said. "I don't know any other way to say it. Double wow!"

"Should I go ahead and send out the wedding invitations?" Sam asked.

"Don't go overboard, pal. We've just met. Give me a week or two. Why have you been keeping her a secret so long? All the other attempts to get me hooked up with the motley crew and what, you've kept her hidden in the ivory tower all this time? Shame on you. Why didn't you tell me about her before?"

"First, she's mainly Deb's friend and second, well, it's a little hard to explain. You see she was married before. It had a tragic end."

"And what," Larry interjected, "her husband died in a freak accident or something?"

"Something like that."

"Oh, thanks a pant load. Now I feel like an ass. What happened?"

"He was an abusive husband. One night he came home drunk and beat the crap out of her just for fun. He had done the same thing before. This time it went well beyond what he had done in the past. She thought she was going to die that night. She locked herself in the bathroom and he tried to force the door open. She looked around for a weapon, anything with which to try to defend herself. The only thing in the bathroom was a wooden-handled plunger. She tried to bar the door, but he was too strong and he broke the door down using his shoulder as a ram. She braced the plunger against the back wall, and he was impaled with it. He died with the handle of the plunger in his heart and the other end in the toilet."

"You have got to be kidding me," Larry said, shocked by the story.

"Ask her, if you don't believe me."

"How do you ask someone about something like that? I guess I'll have to take your word for it. Sounds as if she might have trust issues with men, now."

"You could ask her if her love life ever ended up in the toilet."

"What? Are you crazy?"

"Gotcha."

"What, the story was a lie? You're a dead man. Where's a plunger?"

"No, the story was mostly true. Really. It happened about two years ago. She's just now getting out again. I mean it. Ask Deb. She went through a lot of therapy because of the abuse. That's why she just now showed up on radar."

"Okay, thanks. You said you didn't know much about her. Now, I don't know what to believe. I *will* ask Deb. I don't think she'd lie to me about something like that. If I find out you are lying to me, I'm going to kick your butt."

"That's a deal. She's as sweet as they come. If I had known at the time about the abuse, I would have saved her the misery and heartache. At least he's one sick bastard the world doesn't need to worry about anymore. Speaking of which, where are we on our case?"

"It's like we're on stand-by to be put on stand-by. We're waiting on more information from Doctor Higdon and then we'll see where that leads us. I don't want to go after anyone without all the proof I can get. If we go unprepared, this could all blow up in our face."

"Well, there is Bubba," Lovett said.

"What about Bubba? How are we going to get him out of the grave, better yet, how do we get him out of my apartment? We need him in a courtroom to tell his story. I just don't have all the answers yet. Everything is still up in the air. Maybe tomorrow will bring us some good news for a change. Let's just enjoy today and have some fun. It's a beautiful day, we have two beautiful girls with us, and we're going to a ballgame. What could be better?"

"You could fall down and break your leg and I could go to the ballgame with two beautiful girls by myself."

"Or, I could tell Debbie that you're having an affair with Doris and that Bubba was your lovechild. I'm sure that would go over well. Does she still sleep with that gun under her pillow?"

"Okay, you win round one." Sam laughed. "Let's grab

the girls and go before traffic gets too bad. You should have worn shorts, dummy."

"No way. My legs are not something I want on display when I want to impress a girl. I think I look just fine, thank you."

"Okay, I was just thinking it's going to get hot."

"Hot I can handle. I don't want to get burnt either. I don't need people looking at my legs."

"You mean the way you looked at Connie's?"

Larry turned a little red. "Yeah. You saw that, did you?"

"I think she might have noticed it a bit too. It wasn't real subtle, but it wasn't as if your tongue was hanging out, or anything like that either. At least it was better than staring at her boobs the whole time."

"Didn't you say something about wanting to beat the traffic?"

"Let me grab my glove and cards. You never know who will be signing autographs."

"How many games have we gone to? Ten, maybe fifteen? And how many autographs have you ever gotten? Two. And who were they? I don't remember and I doubt they're still with the team. You're not twelve anymore."

"I got three. But I got them. One even on my glove," Sam beamed.

"A softball glove at that," Larry said, shaking his head as the two walked back to the house.

As they entered the house, Debbie said, "The coolers

packed and ready to be put in the car. Don't forget your glove, Sam."

"Why don't we take my car?" Larry offered. "It's already behind everyone, and it's a little bigger than yours, and besides, I want to contribute to the outing."

Sam was about to say something, but Debbie gave him a stern look, and he said, "Oh yeah, right. Ah, no thanks, Larry, we've got it covered. The parking pass is already in mine and there is stuff in there I might need. You know, stuff like suntan lotion, sunglasses, a brain."

Larry looked at Sam as if he already lost his mind. Sam just closed his eyes and shook his head. Larry knew that was a signal to just drop the subject until he could explain later.

Sam's car was packed and after Larry moved his to the side, he joined Connie in the backseat of Sam's sedan. He saw Sam nod in the rear-view mirror and then he understood. It was so he and Connie could be closer together; matchmaking 101.

William N. Gilmore

CHAPTER 8

The drive to the stadium was filled with jokes and laughter. Everyone was having a good time and there were no thoughts about work or bad things. Larry and Connie were acting like a couple which had been going out for a while. Sam and Debbie were giving each other looks like they pulled something off behind their backs.

Sam pulled into the Blue Lot and showed the attendant his parking pass. He found a space quickly and pulled in. They still had almost half an hour before the beginning of the game. Larry got out, went around to Connie's side, opened her door, and offered his hand to assist her out. She took it and once out of the car she didn't let go. She smiled at Larry and he wasn't about to let go either. Sam grabbed his glove, put it on and made a snapping motion with it at Debbie's butt.

"Looks like bases are loaded," he laughed.

"That's one strike and you won't have any balls if you keep that up," she returned. Everyone laughed, but Sam.

They entered at one of the gates and Sam gave the tickets to the attendant and received the stubs back. He handed out the stubs so everyone knew where they were seated just in case they got lost after going to the restroom, the concession stand, or getting souvenirs of the first date. The seats were between third base and home plate, about ten rows up from the field. They still needed to walk about a third of the way around the inside of the stadium to get to their portal. It was just starting to get crowded.

Before getting to their seats, the girls decided they wanted to make a quick pit stop in the restrooms. Sam and Larry thought that was a good idea as well and they went into the men's bathroom.

"Who did you have to kill to get these seats?" Larry asked.

"You know Lieutenant Withers; works over at Child Exploitation?"

Gillam nodded.

"He also handles security for the stadium. He offered me the tickets after I helped sponsor one of his victims into the Junior Police Program. He's one of the coordinators of the program for the department. He keeps pretty busy."

"I don't remember that. When did that happen?"

"It was several months ago. You weren't involved. It was just something I felt like doing at the time. I wanted to get more involved with kids. Maybe make a difference in their life instead of busting them later."

"Why Sam Lovett, you old softie. There *is* a heart in there somewhere. Good for you. What made you …? Oh, no. Tell me it's not true. Is Debbie pregnant?" He said, grinning.

"No! Not at all. I mean, we're talking about having kids and all. I wouldn't mind having kids. I just want to be careful and find the right time. I want to be able to assure Debbie that I'll be coming home every night. That there won't be a knock on the door by the department chaplain, and she won't be left alone to raise our child."

"There are no assurances, my friend. Anything could happen. You could get hit by a truck crossing the street, slip in the bathroom, or even get hit right between the eyes with a foul ball during the ballgame today. Live for the moment."

"Larry, you're single now. You don't have anyone depending on you every day."

"I've got you."

"That's not the same thing. You know what I mean. Maybe, if things work out with you and Connie you'll see things differently."

"Now don't start that again. You're right, I'm not in your shoes, but don't try to force them on me just so you'll feel better about yourself. I don't know what will happen. I'm a little older than you and set in some of my ways. I don't want kids. This job helps me to understand why some mothers eat their young. Let's just drop it for now. I'm not going to ruin my day with talk of kids. Not yours, and certainly not mine. And don't you dare say anything about kids around Connie."

"You're the one who brought it up; I think. Okay, it's forgotten. Let's go get the girls and get down to the seats. I might be able to get an autograph if we hurry. We also need to get a program, some drinks, and popcorn. We've got a game to win."

"Okay son, just don't spend all of your allowance in one place."

Sam looked up. "Lord help me and save me from idiots."

The girls were waiting for them when they came out. Connie slid her hand into Larry's as they walked ahead of Sam and Debbie. Sam had a big grin on his face and Debbie asked him what they had talked about in the bathroom.

"Shoe sizes," he said.

She smiled, thinking something completely different.

CHAPTER 9

Around noon, Morris picked up King at the BOQ on Ft. McPherson as they arranged. Morris' car was so clean, King wanted to wipe his feet before getting in. Morris even kept a small duster brush up front to keep the dash and console free of dust and dirt.

Both Morris and King were dressed in shorts and T-shirts. Morris wore one with a big VMI on the front of his. King just had the number 7.

"How'd you like VMI?" King asked as they drove to the stadium.

"It was all right. Not my first choice, but it was a family tradition. My father and grandfather went there. A great-great grandfather went there as well, and at the outbreak of the Civil War, he decided to resign and went with the Union side. He was the smart one you might say. Well, maybe not; he was killed at Chickamauga."

I went the OCS route," King explained. "I was the first in my family to be an officer. I guess I just got lucky on some scores."

"The agency recruited me right after graduation," Morris continued. "I thought it would be fun. It gave me a wakeup call as to all the stuff that's going on out there. It's a wonder we haven't started World War III by now, or had a nuclear device go off in the States somewhere. The public just doesn't know."

"And part of our job is to keep the public from ever finding out too much and panicking," King said, "or creating a breakdown to an effective government emergency response."

King continued. "The general has several projects going to confront certain aspects of what is tearing the nation apart. Take the drug war for instance. Millions, if not billions, are spent combating something many of the population want. Television ads aren't going to stop it; slogans won't slow it down; prisons are overcrowded with users, and social programs don't work effectively.

"But that's what we have, for now," Morris stated.

"So, what are we to do instead? King began. "Legalize drugs so everyone who wants can walk around stoned, or get behind the wheel of a vehicle and kill as many as they can? No. Take away their desire for the drugs. How many people do you see who want cancer? None! Have you ever heard of anyone wanting to inject themselves with typhoid or smallpox? I haven't. Let's make the drugs too dangerous to take. Yes, there will be some idiots that just have to have it and then they can be the poster children. Scared straight. Hell, yeah, you betcha."

"Is that what happened with the prostitute and the homeless guy?" Morris asked. "They were given some doctored drugs?"

"No, it wasn't like they were test subjects. We can get

tons of those and have controlled experiments at The Facility. Somehow a batch of treated cocaine got out. It's under investigation by another section. We're the clean-up crew."

"And the general thinks the public will go for this?" Morris asked, a little shocked. "Making the junkies too scared to get high; putting death on the market."

"Okay, let me put it this way," King stated. "If you possessed the ability to stop sixty percent of property crimes; forty to fifty percent of street violence; save billions each year on taxes, not to mention the many thousands of worthwhile lives saved and given a chance to amount to something; what would that be worth? What would you be willing to sacrifice so your children or grandchildren never have to witness a world which is dependent on illicit drugs?"

"There's always going to be something," Morris returned, shaking his head at first, then nodding," there always has been."

"So, if you were an addict, and you knew if you snorted one line of coke, or you took one toke off that joint, and in the next minute you would be stone cold dead, how quick would you be willing to buy a bag from some guy on the street?"

"Jezz, I think I'd run the other way."

"Exactly. And how much would that bag of dope be worth? Zilch."

Morris pulled into a lot where a guy waving a yellow flag was attempting to flag in anyone driving by. He paid the ten-dollar parking fee since he was getting the ticket for the game for free. They still had a walk of several blocks to the stadium.

He hadn't been involved in the current project other than being one of the specially selected security operatives. He didn't know much about what was going on in The Facility and it was specifically designed that way.

He was a soldier. He followed orders and completed the assignments as they were given to him. This was the first he heard in detail of any of the projects. He wasn't sure he felt all that comfortable hearing too much.

CHAPTER 10

The Braves cautiously enjoyed a slight lead on the Dodgers in the fourth inning; four to two. The young rookie was holding his own allowing only three hits. One run was allowed to score on a rare error by the first baseman.

Larry and Connie held hands throughout much of the game and there had been much hollering by both Sam and Debbie. Connie was a big, home-team sports fan, and there wasn't a whole lot she didn't understand about football and baseball. She even knew about the infield fly rule. Both Larry and Sam were impressed.

Larry was a little warm in the pants and drank too much soda to cool down. He needed to make a trip to the bathroom. He asked Sam if he needed to go and Sam reluctantly agreed he did, even though it meant missing some of the action. The girls were fine and Debbie asked Sam to bring back some cotton candy. Connie said she didn't want anything right then and winked at Larry. Larry wasn't real sure how to take that, but her wink and smile gave him some ideas.

They entered the bathroom and Sam finished first. After washing his hands, he told Larry he'd meet him at the concession stand so they could hurry back.

As Larry was leaving the restroom, a man was walking

in, but got held up for a few seconds because of the crowd trying to get in between innings. Larry had to squeeze by and their eyes met when Larry said, "Excuse me."

In that fateful second, Larry saw the face of the phony property clerk and the one on his police identification card. Just as he was about to say something he received a sharp blow to the chin which dazed him and knocked him to the ground. The other man ran off.

There were cries of surprise and confusion from the crowd around him. Some men helped him up, pointing in the direction of the man that hit him. Larry was running after the man before he saw him again. He knew he was wearing a red tee shirt with some white and yellow initials on the front.

He saw a flash of red weaving in and out of the crowd twenty or so yards ahead of him moving at a pretty good pace. He wasn't sure he would be able to catch up with the crowd so thick. Larry tried to maneuver to the outside edge away from the portals where he might move more quickly. He lost sight of the red tee shirt. The man had disappeared into the crowd.

Sam saw some commotion in the large corridor, but was unaware that Larry was part of it until he saw him running through the crowd, away from their seats. He just paid for some cotton candy and drinks, but when he saw Larry running he knew that there was something up, and as a good partner does, he threw everything down and went to get in on the action whatever it might be.

Sam wasn't quite as fast and didn't have the height to be able to see very far and lost sight of Larry, so he did the very next best thing he could think of while still following in the same direction. He looked for a uniformed officer to get a help call out on the police radio.

Morris couldn't believe it. How the hell in a city this size could he run into the one man who knew his face as someone he wasn't? What were the odds? He tried to put him down for a while so he could make his escape, but the cop had an iron jaw and he didn't have position for a solid hit, although the surprise punch did give him a few seconds. He hoped that would be enough.

He didn't know if King witnessed the confrontation, but hoped if he had, he would be able to help him get away. He didn't have a weapon. He didn't think King did either. He didn't want to get caught. There would be too many questions. His best idea was to get out of the stadium as soon as possible. He looked around and didn't see his pursuer, so he slowed down so as not to attract too much attention. People were moving pretty fast here all the time anyway; many being late for the start of the new inning or trying to get to the bathroom after too much beer.

He headed for one of the ramps, but it wasn't an exit. It went down to the field level of the stadium. At the end of one of the portals there were two uniformed cops with their backs to him watching the game. They didn't see him. They didn't look like they were on the lookout for anyone yet. He took out his billfold and removed the cash and stuffed that in his pocket. He then threw the billfold into a trashcan he went by and covered it up. He didn't want to get caught with any identification, even if it was all fake.

He tried several doors which were on that level and after finding most were locked, he found one which opened when he pulled hard enough. It went into a large lighted utility storeroom. There were push brooms, mops in buckets, and other cleaning materials, but there was nowhere to hide in the room. While he was looking around for anything he could use as a weapon, he heard someone try the door. He grabbed one of the push brooms and waited. The door opened and just before he struck, he saw it was King. King looked around to make sure no one saw him enter. He closed the door.

"What the hell is going on, Morris? I saw you hit this guy and then take off running. He got up and started chasing you. What was that all about?"

"That's one of the detectives who saw me at the police property section. He's the one whose identification I used to get into the Crime Lab to recover the evidence."

"Did he follow us here? Does he know about me?"

"I don't think so. We passed in the bathroom and I think it shocked him to see me. I think he's just here for the game."

"Okay, we'll get out of this. Do you have any identification on you, driver's license, military ID, dog tags, anything?"

"No, I dumped it just in case. I know the drill."

"Who else knows you're here? Did you tell anyone you were coming to the game today?"

"No. I haven't spoken to anyone since you asked me. Not even the general."

"Good. We might just get clear of all of this. Check and see if it's clear out there and we'll get going."

Morris started to the door and grabbed at the knob when a thin wire loop went over his head and around his throat. He tried to grab it, but it was already cutting into his skin as well as cutting off his air. King kicked the back of Morris' legs and he went down on his knees.

King put a knee between Morris' shoulder blades, pulling on the thin wire. The wire cut deep as if it were slicing cheese and blood was pouring down the VMI shirt. Morris' hands were slippery with his own blood as he clawed at his throat. Red bubbles gurgled from the large slice left by the wire.

Although he had his teeth clinched and his eyelids pressed shut, Morris saw what looked like a black and white test pattern; then showers of sparkling light that jumped into to a black, bottomless pool; fading quickly like a shooting star; then, nothing. The little resistance he put up ceased and the whole episode was all over within seconds.

King uncoiled the wire around the half-decapitated Morris and let the body fall over. He knelt and used the VMI shirt to clean the wire before it retracted back into the ordinary looking watch he was wearing. He checked Morris to make sure there was not any identification on him as he had said. Only cash and a single car key was on him which King took, saying coldly to deaf ears as he got up, "You won't be needing these anymore." He found a rag on a shelf in the room and proceeded to wipe the inside door handle clear of any fingerprints.

Looking down at the lifeless body of Morris, King added, "When you see your blue coat Grandpa, tell him he should have stayed with Dixie." Using the rag, he opened the door just a crack to see if anyone was around. He opened it wider, looked outside and then stepped out, closing the door behind him and using the rag to wipe the outside door handle behind his back. He dropped the rag and walked away.

CHAPTER 11

Sam finally found a uniform officer and got a call out giving a description of Larry and the direction he was running. He could not give any information on the suspect he had been chasing or why.

Lieutenant Withers and several other officers met with Lovett at the last location he had seen Larry. He gave them as much information as he knew. He tried to call Gillam on his cell phone, but there was no answer. As far as he knew, Larry was still in the stadium somewhere.

He knew the girls would be wondering what was taking them so long, so he called Debbie on her cell and told her there had been some trouble, that they were needed as witnesses, and he would fill her in later. It wasn't a complete lie, but not the whole truth either. He hated doing that, but he was also thinking of Connie. Not the way you wanted a first date to go. Just then, his cell rang. It was Gillam.

"Larry, where are you? Are you all right?"

"Yeah. I lost him, Sam. Somewhere close to the other side of the stadium. He may have taken one of the ramps down or he's hiding somewhere on this level."

"Who? What the hell is going on?"

"Didn't you see him, Sam? It was him! He's still

somewhere close by. I know it. There's not many places he could have gone. I doubt if he got out."

"Larry, will you tell me what's going on. I don't know who you're talking about."

"It was that bastard who pretended to be the property clerk. The one that's on my ID. We've got to find him. We need to set up a perimeter and block all the exits."

"You're joking? The young guy from Property? Here?"

"Yes. That's what I've been saying, Sam. Get hold of someone from the stadium security detail and get those gates manned. You know what he looks like, so give out the BOLO. I'm still looking for him."

"I'm with Lieutenant Withers now. Tell me what he's wearing and I'll get it out right now. Is he armed?"

"I don't think so. All I saw was a reddish T-shirt with some yellow and white initials on it. One might have been a big V. I don't know if he's wearing shorts or pants, and I don't know the color. Nothing about the shoes either."

Sam gave the description to Lieutenant Withers and it went right over the radio. All units were to report in if they made contact, but not to approach the suspect unless he attempted to leave the stadium.

"You wouldn't happen to have the picture of that ID, would you?" Sam asked.

"Not on me."

"Too bad. That would have helped. What section are you

in?"

"I'm around 219. I don't know if he went into the seats or one of the other levels. I don't even know if he's alone."

"Stay where you are until I get there. I'm on the way. It won't be long and I'll have some back up with me. Don't go looking for him on your own now, Larry. Promise me. Let's be smart about this. If he's still here we'll get him."

"I don't know, Sam. He's a professional. He's trained. Either military or some spook shop. We don't have enough officers to cover everything and there's too many people here. There's going to be a rush before long when the game is over. If I wanted to get out without being noticed that's when I would make my move."

"And I bet there's a thousand guys who fit the description," Sam added. "But if we get lucky, we might find this guy and get some answers."

Sam and Lieutenant Withers quickly got around to section 219 and found Gillam looking over a railing, keeping an eye on the fans moving around like ants on a lower level. There had been no sightings of the suspect and the game was almost over. The crowd was getting heaver by the minute. Everyone heading for the exits.

"Still no sign of him anywhere," Sam said. He saw the red mark on Larry's chin. "You okay?"

"Yeah. He sucker-punched me when I first saw him. You should have seen how big his eyes got. Like a dear in headlights.

But I'm the one who froze. Hey, Lieutenant Withers. Thanks for the help."

"No problem. Lovett filled me in on some of what is going on. I've got about fifteen officers I can spare right now to help search, but once the game is over, I'm afraid I'll have to pull most of them for other duties. It's in the eighth now. You say you lost him in this area?"

"That's right. I wasn't right on his tail, crowd was too big. I don't know for sure, but I think he went down the ramp to the lower section. Doesn't everyone, but the players and staff, have to come up those ramps to exit?"

"Mostly. I'll have several of my officers man those exits and start a sweep in the area. No one gets out unless they are known."

"Good. If there is any question about someone's identity, Sam or I can make a positive identification on the suspect. He may be with someone. If so, they are to be detained as well for questioning. Assume he is armed, or at least, trained in self-defense."

Lieutenant Withers got on his radio and started barking out orders for the deployment of his security force. Within just a few minutes, all the posts were covered. A check of all areas began starting on the lower level.

"Lieutenant, are there any security cameras at the entrances or in the concourses which might have captured the suspect?"

"I'm afraid the only cameras are the ones on the ticket booths and the ones in the souvenir shops. They are on digital recording devices. I'll see about getting you copies of today's sells. You might get lucky."

There was a huge yell from the crowd inside of the stadium. One of the Braves hit a homerun in the bottom of the eighth inning making the score six to two. The game was sure to end soon and Gillam was afraid he would lose the suspect in the crowd. He and Sam went to one of the main exits along with the lieutenant as most of the fans anticipating the win wanted to make an early exit to avoid the traffic.

"Sam, why don't you call Debbie and tell her and Connie to meet us here. I really hate having to do this, but I'm afraid I'm going to have to give Connie the brush off for the rest of today. I just hope she gives me another chance."

"If she knew how important this was she wouldn't give it another thought," Sam encouraged. He pulled out his cell to make the call. Larry kept his eye on the crowd as they exited. He thought he saw several people which could have been the suspect, but on closer observations he found he was wrong. Close, but no cigar.

Debbie and Connie walked up. Debbie went over to Sam and Larry approached Connie. She looked at his chin with some concern.

"I don't really know what to say, other than I'm sorry I ruined the day," he said sympathetically.

She smiled at him. "So, you thought that poem up all by yourself in an attempt to say you're sorry?"

He hadn't realized he had made a rhyme. He looked almost shocked that she would think he had at a time like this. His mouth began to open to explain. "I'm—,

"That's not good enough," she said, shaking her head and taking his chin in her hand. "I expect you to spend a little more time with me on the next date." She leaned forward and kissed his chin. "I'm sure you have a good reason for what's going on and I'm ready to hear it when you're ready to tell me. Right now, it seems you're busy with this, and Debbie and I don't want to get in your way, so she suggested we grab a cab and go back to her house for now."

Larry was almost overwhelmed. "Thank you. It's not always like this, I swear. This is just so important right now. Not saying you're not. I mean, well, what I mean is, I do want to see you again, and I would love to spend time with you. Things are so crazy right now, Sam and I are—,

She put one finger over his lips. "Don't explain now. If it needs an explanation, it will come at the proper time. You do what you have to do for now. Stay safe, put all your mind and heart into it. When you're done with this, I hope I'll get the same."

He looked at her with admiration. "One day I hope you'll tell me how you became so understanding and patient. I don't think I've ever met a woman like you. I wish—,

Lieutenant Withers interrupted them by saying, "We've found him!"

CHAPTER 12

Having sent the girls on their way, Sam and Larry followed Lieutenant Withers down a ramp to one of the portals where several officers were standing by. There was a door open and when they looked in, they saw the body of a man on the floor.

He was mainly on his side with his head pulled back. There was a lot of blood on the floor around his head and chest. It was still wet. There was also a lot of blood on his hands. He appeared to match the description Sam had given and he was wearing a red T-shirt. Larry got down and looked closer at the body and confirmed it was the suspect. It looked like his throat had been cut. Sam agreed it was the same suspect who had posed as the property clerk.

"Damn! It looks like someone tried to turn him into a Pez dispenser," Sam said. "Who would be after *him*?"

"We need to cordon off the area here," Gillam said. "I want Doctor Higdon to come out here before anything is touched. Lieutenant Withers, you can call off the search."

"What about whoever did this?" the lieutenant asked.

"We don't know who did this, or why. I doubt we'll find any witnesses. We have a good idea about the time. From the time I saw him last until he was discovered was about a half hour or so. Who found him?"

"Officer Zimmerman, here," Withers said.

"How did you find him?" Gillam asked.

"I was checking the area for the suspect who was put over the radio and I checked this door, you know. It doesn't lock good. You can pull it open if you tug hard enough, you know. There's not much in there. Some cleaning stuff. Mops and brooms, you know. It's not like there's valuable stuff to steal, you know."

"Did you see anyone hanging around or walking away from the area?"

"No."

"Did you touch anything?"

"Hell, no! I didn't even go in there, you know, not with all that blood."

Several of the other officers laughed at that. Odds are none of them would have gone in either. Some to respect the crime scene. Others, the same as Officer Zimmerman; too much blood; still others just wanted to see what was going on.

Lieutenant Withers had sent an officer to the security office to bring back a roll of the yellow crime scene tape. They put the tape up at both ends of the portal and officers were posted at each end with instructions not to say anything.

Gillam got on the phone and called the Medical Examiner's Office. He was surprised he got hold of Doctor Higdon himself on a Sunday. He told him what he had. The doctor said he could be there in fifteen minutes.

King followed the crowd and had made it outside the stadium without any problems. With so many people going in the same direction, it was hard to tell if he had been followed. He didn't think he would have been, but training made him check and take precautions.

He made his way back to where Morris parked the car. The single key opened the driver's door as expected. He got in and sat there for a second, watching some of the crowd go their own way, as he tried to figure out what he was going to say to the general about Morris.

The key fit the ignition as well. He began looking around inside the car. In the glove box were maps, pens, a flashlight, and the registration in Morris' fake name. There was nothing under the seats or dash. No hidden switches or devices and the only thing visible was a black umbrella in the back seat.

King opened the glove box one more time and was about to push the small yellow button which would electronically open the trunk. He stopped. Why would Morris have the umbrella in the back seat? The weather had been nice for days and no threat of rain for over a week. Someone who kept their car as clean as Morris would have kept the umbrella in the trunk while it was nice.

He got out and checked the flow of people one more time. Nothing caught his attention right away. He went to the trunk. The key didn't fit the lock. He got back in the car. He put the key back into the ignition switch, closed his eyes and turned the key. The car started right up and the powerful engine purred. He drove out of the lot and headed away from town making sure there were no tails.

After driving for a while, King got to an area where there was a do-it-yourself car wash. He pulled into one of the unoccupied bays and got into the back seat of the car. He pulled the bottom of the seat out and then the backrest. Behind the backrest and affixed to the firewall were two boxes about the size of chocolate tins. They were shape charges. Designed to blow in a certain direction.

He was sure there was some sort of projectiles set to blow towards the front of the car. Something like claymore mines. Maybe ball bearings the size of small marbles were meant to kill whomever if the explosion didn't get them. He was sure if he had pushed the yellow button he would look like burnt Swiss cheese dipped in ketchup about now. *Cleaver of Morris*, he thought. Not the standard type of theft protection, but very effective.

He retrieved the flashlight from the glove box and used it to search the trunk through the holes in the firewall behind the rear seat. Although the batteries in the flashlight were already weak, he could see in the fading light wires for the device which he believed went to the electric switch for the trunk lock.

He also saw a black briefcase. He was sure the briefcase held documents which would be trouble if they got into the wrong hands.

Maybe this is why there was extra protection. He thought he might be able to reach it, but it wouldn't fit through the firewall holes and he was sure it was locked.

He had to get the trunk open without using the electric opener. He also needed to get it open without blowing himself up. If only he had that damn key. He was sure the key was the by-pass for the device.

He was also sure there was a failsafe, and didn't think cutting the wires or disconnecting the battery would set it off. Protecting the occupant of the car if it was accidently hit in the rear? He still didn't want to take that chance. Morris must have dumped the key along with his ID. There was no way he was going to be able to get back to it even if he knew exactly where he had dumped it. The stadium was now off limits. Too dangerous.

King knew he would have to call the general soon and give him some of the details. He wasn't worried about his actions. Morris had become a liability. He did what had to be done. He couldn't let Morris be captured. The general was sure to agree.

William N. Gilmore

ı

CHAPTER 13

Doctor Higdon arrived at the stadium and was escorted to the storage room where Gillam, Lovett, and Lieutenant Withers were waiting. The crowd had been ushered away from the area and out of the stadium. As far as they knew, there had been an accident, a fight, or possibly even a robbery. An information blackout was ordered and information was not being given out right then. A cover story would be used when the time was right. A crime scene unit also arrived, but nothing was done until Doctor Higdon said it would be.

Doctor Higdon brought two new orderlies with him who rolled a gurney to the location. Both were on a list of students wanting to make a little extra money or extra credit. They looked like they may have been linebackers on the football team. Neither were told any details of the investigation or the ME's Office involvement. He told the detectives that he had left Jaccob to watch over the office.

Gillam and Lovett got the doctor to the side away from everyone and gave him the low down on what had happened up to this point. He looked at Gillam's chin and gave him a lecture about trying to stop someone using his face.

Doctor Higdon entered the supply room, careful of any trace evidence which may still be there. The doctor made a quick examination of the body. It was quite evident that he was dead and from the clean circular cut around the throat someone had used a wire of some kind, as a garrote, wrapped around the man's head.

Two thin, straight lines of dried blood were on the back of the shirt. Doctor Higdon surmised that this was where the killer had wiped off the wire, something he kept with him, or took to dispose of later. It appeared to be a professional job.

Although the hands were covered in blood, there did not appear to be any slices or other defensive wounds there. No time to get the hands under the wire before it began its lethal work.

The doctor came out and gave his findings and what he surmised may have happened. Obviously, an attack from the rear while the man had been standing, and then he fell, or was knocked down, and the slice began an upward cut. Someone else had been in the storeroom. Someone the deceased knew and could turn his back on. Or, so he thought.

"So, you believe he wasn't alone?" Lovett queried.

"Not in that storeroom anyway. That's where he died. Right there. And he didn't commit suicide. There's nothing on him; no ID; phone; papers; jewelry; nothing. And it's not a robbery, it's an assassination."

"When I saw him running," Gillam recalled, "I didn't see anyone with him or anyone else running. I can't say for sure if he was alone, but it's obvious that someone either followed him, or caught up to him, and didn't want him going any further. Maybe so he didn't get caught or identified. The person who did this must have known what activities our 'John Doe' was into, or had orders to take him out from someone who did."

"We need to get him identified as soon as possible then," Lovett said. "Someone will be looking for him. There's no way to keep this quiet for long."

"Go ahead and have your team process the storeroom," the doctor said. "I'll get the body loaded up and back to the office. I'll start on getting him identified."

"But be careful, doctor," Lovett added. "If they killed Kim to get the body of a homeless guy, and broke in to the ME's Office and booby-trapped it, then there's no telling what they might do to get this one back."

"He's right," Gillam said. "You want us to go with you?"

"Thanks, but I think I'll be all right. Another reason I have these two big hulks with me. Plus, I have Betsy with me."

"Betsy?" Lovett questioned the doctor.

"You have someone else with you now, doctor?" Gillam asked.

Doctor Higdon lifted the right side of his jacket and there was a .44 Ruger Black Hawk holstered to his side.

"Meet Betsy," the doctor said, with a big grin. "The only woman I know who is louder than I am and gives just a little bigger kick."

"Holy Wyatt Earp," Lovett exclaimed. "Did I ever apologize for rubbing you the wrong way, doctor?"

"That's some firepower you have there, Doctor Higdon," Gillam said. "Excuse me for asking, but are you ready to use it? Don't you have an oath or something which says 'do no harm'?"

"Son, if I wasn't, I wouldn't bother with it. As for doing no harm. Well, I believe before taking care of others, I must take care of myself first, or I won't be able to help others. If there is someone out there trying to keep me from doing that, then I must deal with them. All for the greater good you see."

"Oh, my God," Lovett exclaimed, "another Vulcan."

CHAPTER 14

Azira rounded up as many of his geek buddies on his computer network as he could contact that Sunday morning. He put out a plea for help in solving the problem of locating Jenny.

Several suggested things he had already tried and several suggested things which could get Jenny in deep trouble, or even put her in danger. These were last resort suggestions. He needed something which would allow him to pinpoint her without anyone suspecting that she was in contact with anyone or assisting her with her own rescue.

One of Azira's buddies, a whiz kid who loved history and computer combat war games, primarily World War II type, came up with the best idea yet.

He recalled how during the war in the Pacific, the United States Navy's Combat Intelligence Unit, having already broken much of the Japanese secret code used for its messages, fooled the Japanese into revealing the code name used for Midway Island.

They sent out a fake message stating Midway Island's desalinization plant had broken down and was out of fresh water. A Japanese message was intercepted revealing 'AF', was out of fresh water, and 'AF' was therefore confirmed as Midway Island. The battle of Midway broke the Japanese Navy's back and saved what was left of the United States Pacific fleet because they used Japan's own information against her.

The gamer suggested instead of trying to break any code, Jenny put in a request for a specialized computer part or other hardware which she needed at her work site. Something only she would be able to use. One that could be ordered and traced from its origin to the location where Jenny was located.

Something which would come from a private company that shipped orders using a commercial delivery service like UPS or FedEx. One which could be traceable without any government involvement.

It was simple, quick, and should be effective. He just had to get the information to Jenny and have her follow through with the plan. What part should be ordered and through whom, for the trace to work, was something else to work on, but that would be a piece of cake compared to all the other stuff.

Azira was starting to feel good about his chances of finding her. Getting her out was something else.

Sunday was Jenny's usual day off, however, she was always on call. There wasn't a lot to do except watch movies or read. There was a new game room where there were some pool tables and a card table, but that wasn't her style. There were also a couple of vending machines. They were free and no money was ever needed.

Tables and chairs were scattered around the room. There

were different board games and a television showed movies 24 hours a day. It reminded her of the rec room for the crazies in *One Flew Over the Cuckoo's Nest.*

She preferred the privacy of her own room; even if it was as boring and depressing as a room could be. It was hers. She decorated it with cut-outs from magazines; which was funny, because the magazines they had access to already had cut-outs. Some articles, pictures, and even some covers were missing from a lot of the magazines. And it was just like a doctor's office; all of them appeared to be several years old.

She never thought there would be a time, but she couldn't wait to get back to her console. Not that she wanted to get back to work. Just the opposite. She wanted to see if there were any more messages for her. She not only wanted the outside contact, she wanted someone to help her get out of The Facility; get back to her parents, and her life. She also wanted to talk with the guy who called himself "The Magician". She was intrigued and thankful all at once. Maybe even a little more than intrigued.

William N. Gilmore

CHAPTER 15

King drove around and found a hardware store. He figured that he could cut through the rear firewall and retrieve the briefcase. It might take a while, but it was the safest way to do it.

He went in and bought a hacksaw and several blades, as well as a hammer and some pliers. On the way out, he remembered to get batteries for the flashlight. He was waiting to call the general until he could secure the briefcase and any sensitive papers, and take care of the car. He didn't want anything pointing back at them.

He drove around and found a small used car dealership which was closed where he could park the car without anyone noticing it. No prying eyes and little traffic for the weekend.

He got back to the rear seat to begin the work of sawing through the metal barrier. He put the hacksaw together with one of the sturdy blades he bought.

He wanted to take another look in the trunk and got the flashlight. When he flipped the switch, it barely had enough light to tell it was on. He opened the new package of batteries and then unscrewed the back of the flashlight and dumped out the old ones. The old heavy batteries came out and hit with a thud. But there was something else that came out as well. King picked it up. He just stared at it a second and then began to laugh. It was a key.

King got out and went to the rear of the car and inserted the key into the lock. No problem. He gave some pressure and the key began to turn. He gave it more and there was a pop which startled him. The trunk had opened and lifted a couple inches.

He gingerly reached his hand in and felt along the opening to see if there were any wires or devices present he hadn't seen. There were none. He bent down and did a visual check using the newly refreshed flashlight. Not seeing anything, he opened the trunk a little more. Still nothing.

He raised the trunk slowly until it was fully open. He had full access to it then. He made a check around the briefcase and made sure it was not attached to anything. He scooted it to one side and found nothing underneath it.

The briefcase appeared to be just a standard one. It had a small combination lock under the swivel handle. It was set at triple 0's.

King wondered if this was another trap. He put his finger over the right brass lock catch and then pushed the slide unlocking device. The catch gave and he let the latch up slowly. He did the same with the left latch. The briefcase was unlocked.

He opened it just an inch and ran a finger along the opening, just like he had checked the trunk. No need to get in too big of a hurry now and get blown to pieces. Nothing. He opened it a little wider.

He could see inside it now and there were no wires or devices. He opened it up.

Inside were folders and papers along with a nice Sig Sauer 9mm with a silencer attached. He removed the folders and underneath them were several passports. Each had Morris' picture, but with different identities. There was a large envelope with driver's licenses, credit cards, and other personal papers to match the passports. Another envelope contained a large amount of cash. All Benjamin's.

There was one more large envelope which caused him to do a double take. On the outside of the envelope was one word. 'KING'. The envelope had been sealed at one time, but was now open. Inside was a folder. He took it out and opened it.

The very first thing he saw was himself. A picture which had been taken for his military identification card. King was not one who was shaken easily, but his hands trembled as he lifted the picture to see what was underneath.

There were several more photos. All of him. Walking; beside his car; in his car.

Also in the briefcase was a handwritten note. A note that wasn't signed. It didn't need to be. He recognized the handwriting. General Cunningham's. The note was short and to the point.

If the need arises, remove loose ends

King was bewildered, mad, and scared all at once. *Why?*

He asked of himself. What could he have done to warrant this? He hadn't been compromised like Morris. He wasn't a screw up like that idiot police lieutenant. He followed orders; he did what was asked of him; he went far beyond.

He had to get to the bottom of this. Now that he knew he was in danger of ending up like Morris, did he dare make contact with anyone within the operation? There was nowhere else for him to go now. Nowhere to hide. He had to know why and he needed to hear it from the general himself. He used to trust the general. Looked up to him.

He needed a plan. Something believable and convincing, not only to the general, but to anyone else who might be looking in. At least for now. He was military. He couldn't just disappear on his own. Although he had training, he wasn't a deep-cover operative like Morris, with all the fake identification and contacts. He was a general's aide. He was expendable.

Morris' death was sure to throw up some red flags now. He had to call the general soon or there would be even more suspicion coming his way.

After sitting there for some time going over and over the possibilities, he took several deep breaths and got his cell phone out. He took several more and then punched in the number that would change the game forever.

CHAPTER 16

Doctor Higdon was conducting the autopsy on the body from the stadium. The fingerprints had been sent through the FBI's Integrated Automated Fingerprint Identification System, usually referred to as AFIS, but nothing had come back yet.

Other than some bruising in the back, between the shoulder blades, on the knees, and a bruise behind one of the victim's knees, there was nothing else remarkable about the body, except the young man had been in excellent physical condition.

There were no gunshot or stab wounds, and there were no defensive wounds on the hands, although both were covered with his own blood. Doctor Higdon found that his first suspicions were correct in that the man had been attacked with a wire put around his throat, from the rear, as he was standing. Pressure was applied on the wire, cutting into the neck and through the layers of skin.

There was a small space in the back of the man's neck which had not been cut, showing the wire was not a full loop, but was a single strand. Most likely, the attacker used two hands in a crisscross method

It was believed that the attacker, while pulling on the wire, kicked the back of the victim's 's knee, forcing him down on both knees. While pressing a knee into his back, the attacker standing over the victim, then pulled upwards on the wire, causing the direction of the wire to be carried just below the hyoid bone into the epiglottis and larynx, almost all the way to the vertebrate. The vertebrate, some muscle, tissue, and a small flap of skin were all which kept the head attached.

The man's clothing was also examined and there were no indications of any other bodily attack. The two thin lines of blood were believed to be where the wire was run through the cloth to get the blood off. There was no identification on the body, but the attacker had left one clue.

The young man had been wearing a shirt with VMI on it. Virginia Military Institute. Not something which was usually worn to a Brave's and Dodger's baseball game by a fan. Maybe the property of a student or a former student.

Estimating the possible age of the young, dead man, Doctor Higdon believed he was between twenty-two to twenty-seven years of age. The latter was pushing it a little. He thought the man was more like twenty-five.

How had he become involved with what was going on? Whom did he work for, and why? As soon as the fingerprints came back he would be able to check a little more in depth.

For now, the body was just another piece of a larger, unanswered question. Every piece just continued to make the question bigger without any hint as to what was truly going on.

Doctor Higdon had to agree with the detectives that

everything appeared to be connected in some way. This puzzle had too many missing pieces and all the shapes were wrong to make a good fit. And the picture, whatever it was going to be, was sure not to be pretty.

Doctor Michaels walked into the room with a look which Doctor Higdon knew.

"What's on your mind, Adam? You look like a first-year med student trying to figure out what bones there are in the body by playing that game, *Operation.*"

"I'm re-running tests on that subject Granger which I did a little earlier. The one who supposedly died from accidental asphyxiation. The detective you're helping had some specific things for me to check out and I'm not sure, but I think he may be on to something."

"How so? What did you find?"

"Granger had a mixture of food and liquid in his mouth and upper throat. To be more precise, he had part of an anchovy pizza and bourbon in his airway, but the esophagus and stomach contents showed only small traces of the pizza. Mainly it was whiskey, and a lot of that," the doctor stated.

"He didn't appear to have chewed or swallowed hardly any of the pizza. Tests show he was lactose intolerant, and had allergies to seafood, as well as to the acids in certain foods, such as tomatoes and onions. He wouldn't, or at least shouldn't have been eating a pizza to start with. His blood-alcohol level showed to be about 2.8, and it couldn't have gone much higher. He would have been at or near an unconscious state."

"Maybe he was too drunk to know what he was putting in his mouth," Doctor Higdon suggested. "Maybe the first bite triggered the reaction for him to vomit. There could be several reasons."

"That's why I made some more tests," Doctor Michaels continued. "I found a very slight bruise pattern around the face and nose of Mr. Granger as if someone had applied pressure with something. I've seen a similar pattern before. It was a nursing home mercy-killing of a lady who had Alzheimer's disease. The husband couldn't stand to see his wife of 60 years be taken away like that. She had already forgotten the children and most days, didn't know who he was," he said, shaking his head.

"She was losing the battle within her mind. He did what he thought was best. It was the same type of bruising pattern. I think someone smothered Mr. Granger with something like a pillow or cushion. The pizza had been put in his mouth to make it look like an accident."

Doctor Higdon looked at his new Assistant Chief for a few seconds and then spoke. "Okay Adam, you finish your tests. You put down your findings on the report and you put down the cause of death based upon your examination. This one is all yours. If it was an accident, then so be it. If it was something else, then make sure you have everything covered. Don't go off halfcocked with just what you believe. Have proof, or at least, something to back up your report. Your name is on it. And your reputation may be riding on it as well. However, I want you to hold the report until I give the word to release it."

Doctor Michaels frowned and turned to leave, feeling like he was being tested himself. He didn't want Doctor Higdon to think he had made a mistake making him the Assistant Chief. Even with all the respect he had for him, for a minute, he was afraid Doctor Higdon would let him hang out to dry if he made a mistake.

"Oh, and by the way, Adam," Doctor Higdon called out to the young man, while he continued his work. "Just to let you know." A smile coming out which he hid from his assistant. "I thought it was a homicide from the get go. Nice work."

Jaccob walked into the exam room and gave Doctor Higdon a startling report.

"There be five more calls with people dead like the girl and the older man in the house."

William N. Gilmore

CHAPTER 17

Azira didn't think of himself as a hero. He sure didn't want to end up as a dead one. He wanted to be like the one at the end of the movie who got the girl.

A plan had been formatted. There were just a few minor things to work out. It needed to go smoothly, quietly, and most of all, safely. Jenny needed to be contacted again and made sure she knew her part. After that, well …, that's when the real fun started. The dangerous part.

He was safe behind his computers and he was sure he had covered his tracks up to now. Most of what he had done on the computer in the past may have gotten him in some trouble or maybe even some jail time, but now, he was about to start the biggest gamble he had ever undertaken. Not just for him; others were involved; others who could get hurt, or even worse.

This was not a time to show off or take things too lightly. Now was the time to grow up, take responsibility, and do the right thing. He was doing all of that, for a change.

Azira made the final set-up on his end for this part of the operation and sent Jenny her coded instructions within her secret back door. He hoped it was still secret. He waited as patiently as he could for her acknowledgement that she understood what she was to do. Everything depended on this part of the plan. If this failed, then like a line of tipped dominos, everything else would fall. They had one chance to get this right.

He paced the room. He stared at the computer and monitors. He didn't dare leave, because if he did, something surely would go wrong; something would break down. He found at times he held his breath. He would wring his hands. He went over the plan in his head a thousand times, trying to make sure everything had been thought of, knowing it hadn't, and fearing his door would be kicked in any minute by an armed S.W.A.T. team.

He looked at his watch. How long had it been? Ten, twenty minutes. It seemed like all day. He looked over at a calendar with pictures from the Hubble Space Telescope. His shoulders sagged.

"Crap," he said, out loud to no one. "It's Sunday. She may not even be at her computer until tomorrow morning." He still didn't want to leave his computers. Maybe somehow, she would see the message anyway. He sat down and stared at the screens until his eyes closed and his head lowered to his chest. He dreamed.

It was like the last scene in *Star Wars*. He was being hailed a hero. The beautiful Princess was putting a medal around his neck, everyone was cheering. Azira smiled in his sleep.

He turned and started to wave to the multitude of fans when there was a crash. Men in black helmets, fatigues, and masks stormed into his room and opened fire on him just as he stood up. The guns never seemed to run out of bullets as his arms and legs jerked and swayed. For some reason, he didn't crumble into a pool of his own blood.

Doctor Higdon stared with bewilderment at the AFIS results on the computer screen. Throughout his years, he had received many results on fingerprint searches since the AFIS system went into effect. There were quick results on most. Negative results on a few. Even a couple which had been misread. There was even one who had his fingerprints removed by acid, but the scars left behind were just as good as regular swirls and loops. But he had never received any notice like this.

The report stated the file was, *CLASSIFIED*. It didn't give any other information. No one to contact; no telephone; no agency; not even a kiss my ass, thank you, and goodbye.

It was already getting late when Lovett drove Gillam back to his house to get his car. All along the way, the two talked about the things which happened over the last couple of days. It was hard trying to put it all together and make every piece fit. One thing they knew for sure was that there was a whole lot more to all of this than met the eye.

This had turned out to be the strangest and most dangerous case they had worked on yet. They both agreed that they didn't want any more like this and hoped there would be no more surprises along the way. Yeah, right.

Sam called Debbie to let her know they were on the way and to fill her in on what was going on so far. She said that Connie had left due to having classes early in the morning, but left instructions to give her number to Larry along with the reminder of a make-up date.

"Looks like you used the right bait," Sam laughed. "Now all you have to do is set the hook and reel her in, nice and easy."

"I don't think right now is going to be the best time for starting up a relationship," Larry replied. "There's too much going on and I've got babysitting duty at my place for God knows how long. Plus I don't want to put anyone else in any danger."

"Always an excuse," Sam said, shaking his head. "Maybe this is just what you need to get your mind off things. Have a distraction, an escape from your boring life once in a while."

"That's just it. I don't need any distractions right now. I need to focus on all this crap and make sure we get to the bottom of this mess. It wouldn't be fair to Connie, or myself, to not devote the proper time and effort in a relationship. Especially one which has barely begun. I'm sure even your little brain can understand that."

"My little brain is thinking of other things about now, but my big brain is reading you five by five." Sam pulled into his driveway and around Larry's Santa Fe. When he stopped, he looked over at his friend and tried to act positive.

"Let's get a fresh start in the morning and maybe there

will be some answers waiting for us. If not, we'll go out and get them. We'll wrap this up, and then you can have that quality time with Connie, and maybe you can relax a little."

"You know you and Deb are the closest thing I have to family. Besides Cali that is. Thanks for being there for me. Thanks for caring. I know we'll get these bastards and everything will work out. It's just frustrating."

"Like I said, tomorrow. Now get out of here," he said, shaking Larry's hand.

Larry got in his car and drove off as Sam headed into his house. Debbie was there waiting on him with a nice glass of wine.

"You didn't slip him the tongue when you kissed him good night now did you?"

"Not this time, although I did get a nice butt squeeze in."

They had a good laugh at this, but Sam was very concerned with Larry's safety. Both body and mind.

William N. Gilmore

CHAPTER 18

Azira jerked awake with a start. He felt all over and there were no holes, no blood. He was still breathing and his heart was still beating; almost through his chest. That was not necessarily a bad thing. As long as it was still beating.

It was funny for him how things sometimes just jumped into his mind while he was thinking of something entirely different. Out of the blue, he came up with an idea on getting Jenny out. It was a brilliant plan even if he did say so himself. And he did.

He settled down enough after the dream (or was it a premonition?), and once he stopped shaking, and wiped the sweat from his face, he re-sent Jenny the instructions for her, which hopefully, would lead to finding out her location. This time he added a few questions to see if his new idea could be turned into a workable plan. Now all he had to do was wait for her response and follow her lead. It seemed so simple. He wondered what was about to go wrong.

"Yes?" the general said into the secure telephone link with a tone which was indistinguishable between a command and irritation.

"Sir, I need to report the loss of one of our assets," King began. "The asset was compromised, and it was necessary to avoid his capture, and be able to keep the integrity of the mission secure, as well as—,

"I already know about it," the general stated. "What is your status? Are you clear?"

"Yes sir. No witnesses, no video, no evidence. No ID left behind, and asset's vehicle has been secured and will be returned to the garage. There may be some added-on security features, so the vehicle has not been checked and cleared except for the ignition."

"Don't worry about that. We'll take care of it. I need you to report directly to me for a debrief. Be here in thirty minutes."

King answered "Yes Sir" into the disconnected phone. He hoped he had sounded convincing. He went around to the trunk and put everything back the way it had been in the briefcase and wiped it down.

He replaced the rear seat and back rest, and then put the trunk key back into the flashlight, putting it back into the glove box. He then discarded the tools he had bought. He made a check of the vehicle to make sure everything was as it had been before he got into it. He was satisfied no one would know he had been in the trunk.

He made the twenty-five-minute drive back to The Facility. When he arrived, there was someone waiting to take charge of the car. He didn't give any information to the person, just the keys. As far as they knew, he didn't have any information.

He entered the building with a few minutes to spare and went directly to the general's office, where the door was open. It was rare to find the general in with his door open. It was late, and the general was at his desk looking at some files, casual dress and with a fat, Cuban cigar in the corner of his mouth. A cloud of smoke was slowly being drawn up to a vent over the general's head. King knocked on the door frame and the general, taking the cigar out of his mouth, told him to come in and close the door. All this without looking up.

"Take a seat. Seems you had quite a day. Who won the game?"

"What?" King said, caught off guard at the question, hesitating for a second as he walked to a chair in front of the general's desk.

"Who won the ballgame?" the general asked again, finally looking up.

"I ..., I don't know," said King, shaking his head. He sat slowly in the chair, keeping eye contact with the general.

"Oh, well. Doesn't matter anyway, I guess." He leaned back in his chair. "So, tell me what went down?" he said, putting the cigar back in his mouth with a stare which went right through King. The general was very calm and cool. This made King even more nervous knowing the general as he did. Not really knowing him at all, he thought. King felt like he was in the lion's cage. He just didn't know if he was part of the show, or the next meal.

Doctor Higdon called in all the help he could muster at that late hour, off or not, sick or not, and he advised them all to bring changes of clothing and to be prepared to be there for a while. With Jaccob's help, he set up one room just for the bodies coming in and moved all others into the cold storage room.

There was limited space and he contacted the Dekalb County ME to ask if they could handle his overflow. He learned they also had a couple of similar suspicious deaths attributed to overdoses. Clayton County also had a couple. Every location he contacted was full.

A lot of questions were being asked. One ME wanted to know if there was an epidemic of some kind going on. Doctor Higdon assured them there was no communicable disease present and everything happening appeared to be something the victims had ingested in some fashion.

Three of the bodies of the resent five reported were transported to the Fulton County ME's office after Doctor Higdon's assistants had come in and responded to the sites of the incidents. Two were like the previous ones, and one may have been a beating death. All had been within the same general area.

There were still at least two more which were unknown. Both of those had been taken to Grady Hospital and were being kept there for the time being. It looked like keeping things quiet was not an option now.

Lieutenant Jones sat in his apartment like he did most nights; a half- empty bottle of beer in his hand and quite a few empty bottles on the table beside the recliner in which he was being swallowed up. He sat in his boxers not watching the exotic adult movie involving two Asian girls. He had a lot going through his mind

He had gotten involved with some people who were taking advantage of his position and his greed, and now, his well-being. He had tried to prove himself to them. He took some initiative to show them that he could be very valuable to them. They weren't happy. Now, he was scared.

Oh, he enjoyed the money, and took it without complaint, believing in some of the promises about even more money and power. He had been weak. It was his nature; selfish, egotistical, and greedy. Now it was all coming back to haunt him. Still, he wanted it all, but without any consequence; at least not to him.

He didn't mind whom he had to step on; whom he had to threaten or blackmail. He knew things and used it to his advantage when it suited him, or when things got a little hot.

Then there were those who worked against him. Those who irritated him like a pesky mosquito buzzing at his ear. Like that little troll, Lovett, and his know-it-all partner, Gillam.

He should have gotten rid of Lovett when he had a chance, but thought it would be fun to keep him under his thumb for a while. Now it looked like the two of them were causing more problems than they were worth. If he wasn't careful, they might become a much bigger problem for him.

Ah, but he had a plan. He was so proud of himself for thinking this one up. It could be just what he needed to get into the good graces of the people who had hold of his puppet strings.

Moreover, it was funny because he still wasn't real sure who "they" were. He only knew that "they" were the ones which kept the beer and money flowing, and had gifted him with the DVD player, and the large flat screen HD television which was showing the two Asian girls doing things to each other that was probably illegal in most states. He was completely unaware he was being watched through that same entertainment system.

CHAPTER 19

Jenny reported to her station ten minutes ahead of her schedule. She had hurried through a quick breakfast in the cafeteria. Monday mornings were rather busy anyway and she had no friends there with whom to talk, or share gossip with, or anyone with whom to pass the time away.

She was eager to see if there were any messages from "The Magician" before she received her morning assignments or anyone started paying too much attention to her. The guards were already in place, but they had nothing to suspect. She did everything to cover her tracks.

It was almost funny that she had helped to set up the updated computer security system which monitored everyone's computer activity. Everyone's, but hers, that is. If anyone checked, it did give the proper readouts when she was on, but when she was in places that were restricted, it showed her elsewhere in cyberspace. She was good. She was glad that they didn't know how good.

Jenny sat at the console and looked around. No one seemed to be paying her any mind, so she opened her secret site and found the messages and questions from "The Magician", but she was confused about what he was trying to do.

Some of the questions didn't make any sense, but she

made mental notes to check the items he wanted. The plan to order something to be delivered to The Facility didn't sound as easy as it did in the message.

First, she had to come up with something which was unique enough that it wouldn't be on hand, in a warehouse, or able to be delivered by some non-government courier. Then she had to get the general to agree to it. That could cause the whole plan to go south. How could she get him to agree to something like that and still have her hands involved in it? She would have to work hard on that one.

She sent acknowledgement of the message and then exited out of her site just as the floor supervisor came over to her and plopped down a stack of files next to her computer.

"I'm going to need these done before lunch today," the supervisor instructed Jenny, without a smile, a please, a thank you, or even a kiss my butt. Not waiting for any response, she turned and walked away to deliver other assignments. Jenny shook her head. Just another fun day.

Although most of her assignments involved setting up secure procedures for other data bases and computer systems, she had the occasional duty of analyzing data and providing statistical results for scenarios involving everything from nuclear fallout and biological weapons to numerous epidemics and asteroid collisions, just to name a few.

It was almost like playing video games where you tried to see how big a body count you could get on brain-eating zombies before they got you, and how much collateral damage you could cause in the meantime, or how to go about destroying the world economy in three easy steps.

It might almost have been fun if it just wasn't so real. Part of it she didn't understand was that there was little involvement by the government. In some of the scenarios there was no use of emergency personnel or equipment. There was no use of the National Guard or any other troops; there was no Red Cross; no assistance given, or shelter provided. There was no quarantine, and no type of medicine, or medical treatment available for those in need. It made no sense.

It was as if there were no government, or at least, one that cared. It seemed all they wanted was a body count. Like cords of wood stacked up. It reminded her of what the Nazis did to the Jews in the concentration camps.

She wondered how it might come to this. How anyone could come up with something so bad, even the government couldn't help. Unless, the government didn't want to help. If the government were to stand by and just watch for whatever reason. Population control? Racial or ethnic cleansing? Class war? On the other hand, maybe it was something altogether new. Something of which she was now a part.

The morning started off early for John Starling as well. He stopped off on the way in to his office, at the county offices to check on a certain piece of land which held a small wooden and wire structure, barely able to stand on its own.

With the assistance of the clerk, he found the right plat book and located the parcel of land which he was looking for. He wrote the information he needed into his notepad and placed it back inside his jacket pocket. The same jacket pocket where he kept a sealed picture of his son, sitting and laughing on a swing. The same picture that he never went anywhere without. One he would be buried with.

Larry Gillam had an early morning too. Is started with being woken by loud snoring an hour or so before his alarm went off. It got worse from there. His jaw was sore from taking the hit the day before, and he believed a tooth was loose. He couldn't get back to sleep, so he took some aspirin and decided to go ahead and get ready for work. The kitchen was a mess. And what was that smell? He wasn't sure he wanted to know. It could have been anything from food to feet.

He fed Cali and left a note for Bubba to clean up or there wouldn't be any shopping done that week. He couldn't believe most of the food he had bought just a few days ago was almost gone. It would have lasted him close to a month.

Larry drove in to work almost forgetting to check his six, but half way there, after changing lanes a couple times and just barely making it through a few stoplights, he found there were no tails or watchful eyes as far as he could determine. At the office, he caught up on some old paperwork and found some new the lieutenant had left for him to finish up and file. Paperwork which was supposed to have been done by the lieutenant. There was also a package there from Simmons with a note. It was a GPS signal blocker. Neat.

Lovett strolled in a short time later and gave Larry's face the once over. "Looks like that's painful. It's swollen some. Take anything for it?"

"I took some aspirin earlier. Swelling should go down soon enough. Now if I could just take enough aspirin to get rid of this big pain in the butt I just got." Larry said, looking straight at Lovett.

"Oh, yeah? What you going to do about all that swelling back there?" asked Sam.

"I'm going to have it stripped off and made into bacon, and feed it to that slob Bubba, and then I'm going to find his mamma and slap her for having him."

"Well, it sounds like a plan to me. Now tell me. Did you call Connie this morning, or did you roll over and tap her on the shoulder?"

"Sam, would you shut up about that. I'll call her when I can. Don't rush me on something like that, and it's none of your business anyway. We had a good time while it lasted and we'll see where it goes when we both have the time, but right now is not the time."

"OK. I get you loud and clear. I guess I owe Deb on the bet then."

"What bet?"

"I bet her that …, well, never mind for now; it was silly anyway."

"What bet?" Gillam insisted.

"I don't want to jinx you my friend. We'll talk about it later. Here comes the lieutenant now anyway. Looks like he had a rough weekend too."

Lieutenant Jones walked into the main office in route to his own. He didn't say anything to anyone. He did look at the two detectives, and when he looked directly at Sam, Lovett could have sworn he had a smile on his face. Not a funny or a happy smile either. A cruel, sadistic type of smile that you might see on someone enjoying the torture of a small animal or being amused at seeing someone suffer.

Sam knew there had to be something inherently wrong with that man. Surely there was some insanity there somewhere in some close relative. And Sam was sure the rotten apple didn't fall far from the tree. It must have fallen on its head and scrambled the insides around a bit.

Lieutenant Jones went into his office and closed the door. The blinds on the small window overlooking the squad room were already closed. He had barely sat down when his phone rang. The voice on the other end was the one he had come to dread as well as hate. It made him hate himself as well at times, and that was a something which didn't happen very often.

Sam found a large sealed envelope on his desk with his name written on it. There was nothing else written on it. There was no return address and it had not been stamped. He picked it up and it was extremely light and thin. He opened it with a metal letter opener, careful not to tear the flap.

When it was opened, he peered into the envelope and gave a "Huh." The envelope was empty. He opened it wide, looked inside again, and even shook it upside down, but nothing came out. There was nothing inside other than air. He wasn't sure if anything had ever been in the envelope. He called over to Larry and asked him if he had put the envelope on his desk and Larry said he had never seen it before. Sam just shook his head and put the envelope into the wastebasket by his desk.

Lieutenant Jones came out of his office and called for a squad meeting in five minutes. All the day shift units not already out on assignment were there and began heading for the conference room where they usually held their briefings.

After a while, Lieutenant Jones came into the room and began by complaining that the stats for the past month were down. Arrests were way down and seizure totals were a joke. Things were going to get turned around and they were going to start now.

He told the group they were going on a raid this morning. It was a house where drugs were being sold and he used his own informant to make an undercover buy of narcotics before he came into the office that morning. He held up a small evidence bag containing a couple small, zip-locked bags, containing what he said was the cocaine the informant had bought.

"Gillam, I want you to lead the raid, and Lovett, I want you to get the search warrant for the house. When the meeting is over, come to my office and I will give you the information you need. You should have the warrant and get it signed by a judge within the hour. I want everything done before noon. The rest of you will stand by until they return with the warrant and I will give the briefing. That's all for now."

The lieutenant went directly back to his office. Lovett and Gillam looked at each other for a few seconds. There were some grumblings among the other detectives and a few began to raise some questions.

Gillam, the only sergeant in the room and therefore the ranking person there, told the rest of the squad to hold on until he could get some more information. This was not even close to how these operations were supposed to be conducted. Already there were several major things Gillam had problems with. He nodded at Lovett and headed for the lieutenant's office. Gillam knocked on the outside of the closed door.

"Enter," said the lieutenant.

Gillam and Lovett went into the office, Lovett closed the door behind them. Gillam opened his mouth, about to voice his disapproval of how the meeting went and the apparent way the drug evidence was obtained. A clear violation of SOP's.

Jones knew better than any of them that no undercover operation was to be conducted by a single detective without proper backup, and drugs were not to be purchased by an informant unless there were at least two detectives supervising him and taking control of the drugs.

Before Gillam could say anything, Jones started in on both of them. "The two of you are so busy chasing ghosts that I have to go out and do your field work for you. There's so much dope out there right now, it's almost falling off the trees. You can believe me that if things do not improve very quickly it will show up on both of your evaluations. You're lucky I don't have both of you on desk duty right now." He stuck out a piece of paper and told Lovett that this was the address of the drug house as well as the information on the buy he had made this morning.

"Lieutenant," Gillam began. "I don't feel this is the right procedure to obtain the warrant. Maybe it would be best if you write it up yourself and get it signed since it was your operation this morning. We weren't there and don't have all the detailed information."

Jones looked startled for a second and then squinted his eyes at Gillam. "So, you are refusing to follow a direct order by a superior officer, huh? Your commanding officer at that! Are you sure that's how you want to play this out, mister?"

"Lieutenant," Gillam began. "I just want to make sure that there are no loopholes in anything. I don't want us forcing our way into a house, handcuffing people, taking them to jail, and then find out that there was a problem with the warrant; they walk free and then we have a big lawsuit on our hands."

"Gillam, I've been doing this a long time. I tell you everything is solid if your partner there can write the warrant up right."

"Well, I'll write it up right, but I won't lie," Lovett said. "Not for you, or anyone else. I don't care if they have half the cocaine out of Columbia in that house." He couldn't wait to see him behind bars. The clock was ticking.

"I told you what happened. There's the address," Jones said, pointing at the paper in Lovett's hand. "Get it done. Now!"

Gillam and Lovett left the lieutenant's office and Sam went back in a huff to his desk where he quickly wrote up a search warrant from the forms on his computer.

Gillam informed the rest of the squad to get their raid equipment together and stand by until they returned with the signed warrant. He didn't have any other info for them yet. He knew them all pretty well, and that they were dedicated, hard workers; both men and women. And how they felt about the lieutenant. They all knew he was using them to make himself look good and buck for a promotion.

Sam put in the warrant the information which had been given by the lieutenant, careful not to make it sound like he or any of the rest of the squad had had anything to do with the early morning operation.

He was going to have to swear in front of a judge the

information contained in the warrant was correct and factual. He wasn't comfortable with this at all. He wasn't sure how a judge would feel about it either. Most were sticklers about what went into a warrant. They didn't like having problems with paperwork in courtrooms where they could get overturned. It looked bad on their records when they went up for other appointments.

He got the warrant finished and he and Gillam were about to leave to go to the courthouse when Jones poked his head out of his office door.

"See Judge Freeman. I just got off the phone with her. She's expecting you. Then get your asses back here in a hurry so this can get done." He ducked back in his office and closed the door not waiting for any reply.

"Reminds me of prairie dogging," said Lovett.

"Prairie dogging?" asked Larry. "You mean like those western prairie dogs going in and out of their boroughs like you see on the *Discovery Channel*?"

"Well, sort of," snickered Sam. "More like when you have to go to the bathroom really bad and you almost do, but you suck it back in at the last second."

"Now that's gross, Sam. But you know, very appropriate," Larry laughed.

The detectives headed out of the office and to their car. No one noticed Lieutenant Jones coming out of his office, going over to Lovett's desk, and removing a discarded envelope from the wastebasket with a tissue. Jones looked around the office to make sure no one saw him, then he returned to his office.

He made the preparations needed to bring the next part of his plan together. His face made that hideous contortion which he called a smile as he picked up the phone and called another link in his chain of misadventures.

CHAPTER 20

King told the general everything. Well, almost everything. He even included how he had used the watch the general had given him. He thought it had been more of a gimmick at the time he got it, rather than a real tool, but it came in useful when it was needed. He explained to the general that he couldn't let Morris be captured after being recognized and allow the mission to be put at risk. He was sure Morris might be able to evade questions and put off any further risk of exposing his involvement for a time, but maybe only for a time. He felt he had to act.

General Cunningham had agreed with him, which was a big relief. The general even praised him for his quick thinking and his ability to get away himself without detection. He asked about the car and King stated he didn't know anything about it, but knew he couldn't leave it in the parking lot at the stadium. Morris had had only the one key with him.

The general again gave King praise for handling the situation well and had dismissed him for the night. A driver took King back over to the BOQ. He felt better about his position now. He had been scared, but began wondering if maybe he had overreacted. After all, the general was a reasonable man. He demanded respect, but most notably, loyalty. However, Morris wanted it to go both ways as well. He wanted loyalty from the general. What he had found made him question that loyalty. He needed to have some insurance, just in case.

Special Agent in Charge, Tommy McGill entered his office that Monday morning with no expectations of any kind. He never knew what he would find waiting for him. What crisis or what delights might be on the other side of that door were just what the good Lord had planned for him, and there was nothing he could do about it, but accept it, and deal with it the best he could. Today was no exception.

He came in, hung up his jacket, sat at his desk and turned on his computer to check the news, the weather, and his E-mail. There was nothing exciting and the world was still out there this morning just as it had been every other morning for billions of years. The sun still shone, the winds blew, the oceans and seas lapped their shores, and time went by.

Then he checked his voice-mail. He was only half listening, but when he heard a voice say something about an *Operation Back Street*, everything stopped. It hadn't been Azira. This was a voice he never heard before. They didn't give their name, but just began sprouting off some stuff about this operation they had some information on.

They gave a name of a General Cunningham who oversaw it. How it was supposed to be a government think-tank dealing with national security, but General Cunningham had an underlying agenda that was being kept secret from those same government officials, and it was being funded by some CIA or NSA black bag operations.

The voice said there had been some unfortunate deaths which had occurred due to a breach in security and the loss of contaminated product, but didn't give many more details. The voice said he was interested in an immunity deal and witness protection in exchange for detailed information. He said that he would be back in touch soon and he would use the code name Grey Ghost.

Tommy wanted to know how the person had gotten his number, but the big question was how the bloody hell did they know he knew anything about this Operation Back Street. He called Azira right then.

Azira's phone didn't ring. It had more of a techno-heavy metal tone which could wake the dead. Well, maybe piss them off anyway. It didn't matter. Azira was in the shower wearing waterproof headphones, listening to a symphony by Bach. He was conducting an invisible orchestra as warm water pelted the top of his head. He really was a strange kid.

CHAPTER 21

Doctor Higdon was working on another one of the bodies brought in from Grady Hospital at one examining table while Jaccob, who was not too far away, was preparing another. Doctor Higdon's was a young man who had bleed out due to internal organs and blood vessels bursting just like many of the rest he had seen over the past several days.

All the tests they had performed still didn't give them much of a clue about what they were dealing with except that in all the cases it appeared whatever the substance was, it was being introduced through ingesting narcotics. Specifically, smoking crack cocaine.

Jaccob was getting more work experience than he could ever have imagined. He had been very useful and had shown a unique ability to learn things very quickly without having them repeated or explained more than once. He seemed to be a natural.

When Doctor Higdon allowed him to assist during some of the autopsies, he was thorough with his examinations, but did not attempt to rush through them. He treated each body noble and with respect, and surprised everyone that even for his size, he was delicate and nimble.

An orderly stuck his head in the room and told Doctor Higdon that a large box had just been delivered for him and that he had signed for it and put it in his office. Doctor Higdon thanked him and went to the sink to wash up. He removed the surgical gloves he had been wearing and deposited them into the biohazard receptacle, washed his hands and asked Jaccob to finish up with the young man and to call him if he needed any assistance. He didn't think he would.

Doctor Higdon, thankful for the break, went straight to his office hoping the package was the one delivery to the ME's office he had been looking forward to. On his desk was a large brown box. He went over to it, read the return address, and smiled. He grabbed a letter opener off his desk and cut the brown tape sealing the box. He removed several layers of paper and bubble wrap and there it was. *The Bomb.*

Gillam and Lovett had just arrived at the courthouse. Much of their conversation while in route centered on Lieutenant Jones and his behavior that morning and how they needed to wait to show their hand. Gillam had wanted to punch him in his face and Sam, well, Sam was ready to empty one clip into him and reload for another. They needed the drive over to calm down. It didn't work out that way very well.

They went straight to Judge Freeman's chambers and the clerk in the front office had them sit and wait while the judge finished up with another matter. After a few minutes, the judge walked out with three men and a woman. The woman and one of the men carried briefcases and were well dressed. They appeared to be attorneys. The other two men were dressed even better, wearing Italian made suits and shoes.

Gillam recognized one of the two men as being one of the city's biggest known crime bosses who had come under state and federal indictments several times for corruption and RICO violations, but had never come to trial.

Judge Freeman shook hands with the attorneys, but gave the boss a very warm embrace and appeared to whisper in his ear saying something which caused the man to laugh. The other man just stood to the side and Gillam noticed a slight bulge under the well-made jacket. He was packing and must have been the bodyguard.

How the hell did he get in the courthouse carrying a weapon, Gillam wondered. As the group entered the outer office, Judge Freeman told her clerk to show them to the exit. The group left, but not the way Gillam and Lovett had come in. There must be some back way which was less conspicuous, Gillam surmised.

"Are you here from Lieutenant Jones' Narcotics Squad?" asked, Judge Freeman.

"Yes ma'am," said Lovett, both he and Gillam standing as he pulled out the warrant from a file folder.

She took the warrant, walked over to the clerk's desk, grabbed a pen and signed it. She handed it back to Lovett, turned, and retreated to her office. She didn't even bother to read it. No questions; no swearing to the contents of the warrant; nothing.

Gillam and Lovett were left standing in the judge's outer office alone. There was nothing to do, but leave. There would be a lot more to talk about on the trip back to their own office.

John Sterling hung up the phone after the conversation with the owner of the small tract of land on which he had conducted the research. The elderly man, receiving the land as an inheritance, had been holding onto it for many years hoping to sell it to a development or construction company which may want to put houses or apartments on it.

However, with the economy in the tanks now and the housing market almost non-existent in the area, he was happy to take the offer John had made. Besides, part of the offer had been to pay off the taxes on the land which the man had not paid in several years, giving him worry the land would be foreclosed on anyway. Might as well make something on it.

John wasn't looking at the land so much as an investment as to have something to call his own and to occupy some of his time. Call it a hobby or call it therapy, it didn't matter. In his mind, he was making a connection with Curtis, and therefore, he was making a connection with his son and the years which had been stolen away from them.

Sergeant Moore came over to Starlings desk and sat at the chair beside it. "I know you got frustrated with my decision to let Narcotics handle that body over on Griffin Street the other day. Lieutenant Jones told me he was going to have his men handle it because there was no question it was an overdose and there may be some special considerations involving a new type of drug on the streets. He said he was trying to keep it quiet for now. Have you heard anything more about that?"

"I know there has been a large increase in drug related deaths over the past week. I've been working with a couple of Narcotics guys I trust who believe there may be more to the story than just some new drug. I don't think Jones is being straight with everyone. He seems to have his hands in whatever is going on."

"Be careful what you say without proof," Moore cautioned. "You know what they say about walls having ears? I will be there for you. I'll back you up as long as you are right. Don't bump heads with Jones. You may be the one who gets knocked on your ass. He has a lot of brass keeping him out of harm's way."

"He won't always have that protection," John said. "And when he screws up royal, I know a few guys that will be there to make sure the screws are tight and will hold."

William N. Gilmore

CHAPTER 22

Gillam and Lovett returned to their office finding the rest of the squad dressed out in their raid gear and awaiting the briefing by Lieutenant Jones.

Jones came into the conference room not dressed out. He wasn't going on the entry. Of course, not. He was Lieutenant Mark Jones. He didn't get put in danger.

Jones gave a description of the house. He even had pictures from several different angles. He gave detailed descriptions of who might be in the house, to include names and nicknames and the possibility of weapons. The only thing he didn't give was exactly where the drugs were being kept in the house.

Gillam was amazed. The details the lieutenant was giving were from something which might have taken weeks to obtain. In addition, the photos were high quality, detailed shots taken from a high-resolution camera with a telephoto lens. How the hell did he get those? This was not something the lieutenant did on his way into work this morning. Something didn't add up.

The raid was to include two of the four black, unmarked raid vans the squad had. Jones told Gillam to take one team in one van and Lovett to take the other in the remaining van. Jones said he would join the teams on site after entry had been made and the house secured, but there was to be no searching for drugs until he arrived. He was such a leader.

The teams arrived in the unmarked vans with Gillam's team securing the outside and the rear of the house while Lovett's team attacked the front door to make entry and secure the house. The front door slammed as the vans came to a stop and yelling could be heard inside the house.

Two members of Gillam's team raced for the back of the house just in time to capture one young man and a woman trying to run out the back door. The front door had an iron burglar bar door in front and was quickly forced open by two team members yielding a sledgehammer and a halogen tool; just like the ones firefighters use.

Another team member used a one man, heavy, metal battering ram to force open the inner wooden door which had been slammed shut and locked. The ram shattered the door and the doorframe. Parts of the deadbolt lock went flying. The rest of the team members entered the front room in single file behind the front man holding a bulletproof shield. Everyone was yelling 'police' and 'search warrant' while making sure to check left, right, up, and down, for any suspects or booby-traps which might be present.

The line did a leapfrog, checking behind every couch and chair, and every door. They entered each room and checked under beds, in closets, and anywhere someone might hide.

Entering one room, they found a very large man trying to

go out a window, but he had become stuck due to his large size. Besides, there had been a team member waiting for him outside as well. It took three team members several minutes to get him unstuck, and there had been fears they would have to call the fire department to assist.

Once unstuck, it took three sets of plastic flex-cuffs to get him secured. When he was read his Miranda rights and finally questioned, he grudgingly gave his name as Tiny. Go figure.

Lieutenant Jones was radioed and advised the house was secure. He reiterated that he did not want the house searched until he got there, which would be in about five to seven minutes.

If the house was clear he wanted all team members standing by outside. He wanted the suspects processed and held in one of the vans without being able to see outside. He wanted anyone passing by or snooping to be sent on their way. If they refused, then make an arrest on them and put them in a van as well. The lieutenant was being hard-nosed.

All the team members were standing out front of the house except for two who had been placed on guard at the rear of the house. They still had on all their raid gear, including their bulletproof vests, black Kevlar helmets, and black masks, which hid their identities from the bad guys.

It was beginning to get rather hot already that morning as it approached noon. Gillam passed out bottled water from the vans supply to anyone who needed it to include allowing the suspects to have water if they wanted it as well. There wasn't much shade in the area.

Jones pulled up in his car and headed for the house. Gillam met him half way and told him the entry was smooth and there were three people being detained. There were no injuries. No weapons had been found on anyone, and no searching had been conducted per his order.

"Well it's about time you did something right," Jones said, sarcastically.

"I want you and Lovett to do the search. You do remember how to do a search, don't you?" Not waiting for an answer or expecting one, he continued. "I want one team to finish with any paperwork on the suspects that needs to be completed and I want the other team to be released."

"We don't know what charges if any will be made on the suspects. We haven't found anything yet," Gillam said.

"You will," said the lieutenant, confidently. "And when you do, I want you to bring it to me. I need to see if this is what has been killing all the junkies in the area. I'll be taking it for some special tests which the Crime Lab can't make. Is all of this clear, sergeant?"

"What about chain of evidence and the use of it in court?" Gillam asked, wondering what the lieutenant had up his sleeve.

"I'll worry about that, sergeant. I'll get the proper paperwork so your silly, little rules aren't broken and you don't have a hissy fit. Now go in there and find the drugs like a good little doggie and take your Siamese twin with you."

Lovett had been talking with the other team members when Gillam came over and gave the orders as directed by the lieutenant. He and Lovett went into the house where they removed some of their equipment and took off their masks.

Lovett laughed at Gillam when he took his mask off which left his red hair in an almost punk spike fashion. Gillam responded that at least he was glad to have hair to which Sam kept quiet.

They divided the house into two sections and began together in the front room after putting on thin latex gloves.

Under a cushion in a big chair, Lovett found a badly maintained Rossi .38 caliber revolver, loaded with three old, discolored, lead-nosed rounds. It had food and dust stuck to it, as if someone had forgotten for years that it had been there. If it shot, it might blow up, or if a bullet hit you, you would probably die from an infection more than any injury.

Lovett got two of the rounds out easily, but had to poke the other one out because the ejector was stuck with some goop and the bullet had its own crap on it. He finally made the weapon safe and placed it on a table. He wrote its description and the location it was found, with his name beside it.

Also in the front room, in a closet, Gillam found a shoebox with cash stashed in it along with several small bags of crack cocaine. He called Lovett over, counted the money in front of him, and then listed the money by the denominations and the total on the inventory sheet along with the crack. It was a total of $435.00 and twelve five-dollar hits of crack.

They had cleared the front room and moved to the kitchen, which was in the back of the house. This part of the house was nasty with pots and pans and dishes, some still containing food, piled in the sink with dirty water, if it could be called that. Roaches were crawling everywhere.

Lovett, just at the thought of everything there, began to itch and squirm a little. Every little twitch was believed to be a roach crawling on his skin. This was one of the things he hated most about the job.

Gillam opened the refrigerator door and immediately wished he hadn't. The smell that escaped lingered long after he quickly shut the door. He knew better, but everything had to be checked. He had just forgotten to hold his breath. He was glad he didn't have lunch yet. Now, he may not have it at all. Too bad you couldn't package this and sell it as an appetite suppressor for a new diet plan.

There had been some papers and pieces of mail with names on them, but it was easy to see there were many people using this address either as a mail drop or like a rooming house with a very high turnover rate. Some even used it when they were arrested or needed an address for their probation officer.

Gillam moved down a hallway to a bedroom which had an open hasp and lock. He went in and saw there were piles of dirty clothes on the floor and even some on the old bed. An old dresser, matching the bed in a 1970's era style, was cluttered with ceramic figurines, ashtrays and bottles. He first checked the bed and then under the mattress. Under the mattress, he found a Lorcin .380 automatic pistol, loaded with seven rounds in the magazine. Also under the mattress were several porno magazines, adult DVDs and sex toys.

A closet held mostly women's clothing. Clothing suited to an older and rather large woman. Maybe the owner of the house. In the back corner of the closet was an old 12-gauge shotgun. The barrel had lots of rust on it. It wasn't loaded. Also in the closet were numerous old electronics. VCRs, tape players, and an old 12-inch television with the rabbit ears on top. Things which may have at one time been stolen and pawned for drugs. Things which held no real value now. There was even a large sealed box of toilet paper. A brand which hadn't been on the shelves of any store for at least five years.

It always amazed Gillam some of the things you would find doing a search warrant at an old drug house, but surprisingly, too many of the houses he searched were just alike.

You find the same old things. Old guns, broken electronics from the 70's and 80's, roaches, people hoarding things for no reason. It was almost as if they were afraid to throw anything away, believing it might have some value to someone someday soon. Maybe it would, in a few hundred years.

Gillam continued the search of the bedroom and began to

open drawers in the dresser and found each one stuffed with old papers, letters, and more roaches. There was an adjoining bathroom. He went in and was amazed. It was the cleanest room in the house. It was spotless. It even smelled clean. But there were no towels, no washcloths, no floor mats, not even a shower curtain. It was as if it was never used.

Lovett in the meantime made his way into one of the bedrooms and began his search much the same way Larry had. Only in this bedroom, it was obvious that it was being used by a male. In addition, with the size of the clothes there, it could only have been Tiny's.

The bed, which appeared to be a twin size, had a large depression in the middle. There were actually two mattresses on the bed. The waded sheets were discolored and looked like they hadn't been washed in months. They smelled that way too.

Lovett lifted the top one and under it he saw a large clear plastic bag containing dozens of the smaller zip-locked bags containing hits of suspected crack cocaine and another plastic bag containing large chunks of what looked like sugar cookies, but were in fact the larger flat pieces of crack cocaine before they were broken down into the dime and nickel bags. Lovett yelled out "Bingo" to let Larry know he had found something good.

The complete search of the house netted over 130 hits of crack cocaine and another 200 grams of crack which would push the total well into the range for a solid trafficking charge. Include the weapons, with the Lorcin found to be stolen, and you were looking at some very serious prison time. It was time to talk with the suspects; most notably, Tiny.

Gillam and Lovett brought out the items in a box and secured them in the van. Lieutenant Jones looked over the seizures and took the cocaine out.

"Good job you two. For a change. Wonders will never cease. Who would have known that this little rat hole would be holding so much? I'll take the drugs to have them tested and you turn in the weapons and cash. Then I want you back at the office. I want to go over some other locations for future raids with you."

"What happened to the suspects, where's the rest of the team?" Lovett asked, noticing the van was empty and no one from the team was around.

"I had a paddy wagon come and take the suspects to detention so as not to waste any more time. I have Jergens there ready to fill out tickets. Now that we know all the charges, just radio her and she'll get it done."

"We needed to question them," insisted Gillam. "There are things we need to find out. Even simple things like who owns the house."

"Oh, there not talking," Jones said, matter-of-factly. "They all lawyered up. You weren't getting anything out of them and there was no reason to keep them here. I had the rest of the team picked up as well. It's hot and there's no need keeping them out here waiting on you. There's other things needing to get done, you know. Take the van, turn in the rest of the evidence, and get back to the office. Get moving because you're wasting my time now." Jones walked off with the dope and got into his car and left.

"Well, what now chief?" Lovett asked of Gillam.

"You radio Jergens. I'll drive us to property. You know, we're right around the corner from where Jessie died. Lowery is just a couple blocks over and some of the other deaths occurred within a few blocks of here as well. I wonder if this could be the source."

"It's possible," agreed Lovett. "It might be the same stuff, but if it is, how did it get here and how did it get contaminated with whatever is in it? We may never know. Lieutenant Jones took all the dope. For testing, he says. Yeah, right. If he did, I bet we never get a report on what's in it. And who's doing it anyway?"

"I wouldn't be so sure about that," said Gillam, pulling several of the small zip-locked bags containing crack cocaine from his pocket and waving them at Lovett.

"We're getting our own test done. As the leader of the raid team and you being the affiant of the search warrant, we're maintaining a chain of custody on this evidence. This is going right to the Crime Lab and we will put it right in the hands of the chemist. Won't be anyone screwing around with this stuff until we get some answers. I'll write up a supplemental report to cover our butts, but I won't file it with all the other paperwork just yet."

"Sounds like you had a plan already in the making when we did the raid," said Lovett.

"Not until we found the dope and Jones was waiting to get his grubby little hands on it. There is so much wrong with the way things have gone lately. We know Jones is a sneaky, slimy, murdering, son of a bitch and he'll stab us in the back in a heartbeat if it suits him. We have got to be careful and be able to nail his ass for good without anything coming back on us. We have to time everything right, so he has no way of shaking loose and he goes to prison along with anyone who is connected with him and is a part of all this crap. I'm tired of him. We owe it to a lot of people."

"All right," Lovett said. "Now tell me how you really feel."

Lovett radioed Jergens and gave her the information on which she had been waiting. Gillam drove them to the police property section where they tuned the other evidence into a clerk they knew. No mistakes there.

They drove over to the Crime Lab, hoping that there wasn't a GPS bug on the van. Once at the Crime Lab, Gillam met with Mr. Hernandez and released the cocaine to him with a receipt to show the continued chain of evidence.

Mr. Hernandez agreed to make a rush on the analysis to make up for all the confusion from earlier and the loss of the other evidence. He also agreed to release the results only to Gillam or Lovett and not send them to the Narcotics office as was the usual procedure for test results.

Gillam and Lovett left the Crime Lab and hightailed it for their office before Lieutenant Jones began to wonder what had taken them so long.

CHAPTER 23

Jenny had been thinking all morning about what to do to regarding the plan described by "The Magician" and if it was even feasible at all. Everything depended on her selling the ruse to the general. She went over several speeches in her head, careful about things which might trip her up or areas where the general might have some argument. She believed she was ready and called the general's direct line. Having helped set up some of the security procedures, she was one of the few who was allowed to call that number. The general answered.

"General, this is Jenny. I may have an answer to the hacker problem we had earlier. I believe I can track him down if I had access to some specialized equipment and software which was developed by an independent private company. May I come up and talk with you if you have a few minutes?"

"Come up in about five minutes. I'm finishing lunch right now."

Jenny took a deep breath. This was one of those moments that puts a butterfly in your stomach. It was a 40-pound butterfly and each beat of its wings was like a punch to the gut. Her heart raced and she could feel herself sweat although the air conditioning was going full blast.

After waiting for about four and a half minutes, she

slowly began to make her way to the general's office. It took her all of forty-five seconds to get there. She knocked on the open door. General Cunningham directed her to enter and to a chair in front of his desk with a wave and a point.

"Okay, Ms. Jordan, what is it you think you need and why do you need it?"

Jenny began one of her rehearsed speeches. "General, when we had the security breach from the hacker, the system was not set up for an elaborate trace to find out who it was and where they were. We did not anticipate someone even attempting to get into the system much less someone actually getting in."

"I thought you said they didn't make entry into the system, Ms. Jordan?" General Cunningham said, cocking his head a little and his voice rising with each word.

"I said they didn't get into any sensitive areas, general. They got into the mainframe title area only before I shut them down. This was no amateur and the equipment they were using was very up to date and sophisticated. I made sure there were no Trojans or other attachments to our virtual ports and our IP and DNS are secure. I tried a reverse DNS query, but did not get anywhere. What I need is a special trace router to track down this hacker and to locate his base of operation, or at least, get his IP address. I believe the hacker will try again. They're that way. It's a challenge for them. Without the equipment, I may never be able to locate who it is and they may be able to get further than they did before even with all the firewalls and security I have in place."

The general just shook his head. "I am not sure what you just said, but it sounds like you need something to find and stop this intruder. You make a list of what you need, where to get it and how much it's going to cost me and I'll see what I can do. I want to be notified immediately if they try again. Is that clear Ms. Jordan?"

"Yes, sir."

"Do you need any other assistance or additional personnel?" He asked.

"No thanks, general. I work better alone," Jenny said, adding. "Some of the items may be special order. It won't take long and I'm sure it will be reasonable. I'll get you that list and I'll find that hacker for you. You can bet on it."

"You do that, Ms. Jordan. I want to know just where that little pest lays his head at night."

"Me too, general, me too."

William N. Gilmore

CHAPTER 24

Gillam and Lovett returned to their office just as Lieutenant Jones was leaving.

"Took your sweet time with everything. I got called away on something and I may not be back. I want you to finish all the paperwork on the raid. Get the search warrant return signed and filed with the court and have a copy of it and the report in my box tonight. I want to give a full briefing at the commander's meeting in the morning. Don't go out and get yourself shot up or anything. That would break my heart. Be here on time first thing in the morning so we can go over those other operations I was telling you about after my meeting. It's going to be a busy week. It's time you got some real work done."

"Sure," was the only thing Gillam replied. Lovett didn't even respond or acknowledge him. He went straight to his desk, sat down, opened a drawer and took out some files.

Gillam went to his desk and thought about calling Connie. He decided to wait until he got home. He didn't want any eaves dropping which would trigger questions or comments from Sam. Besides there was a lot to do before they got off and he thought he better get started on it. Not for the lieutenant, but because it just had to be done. He wasn't going out of his way to make things easy for him and he wasn't going to be doing any more of that S.O.B.'s work for him.

Doctor Higdon had been thrilled to get *The Bomb*. He got five of them. *The Bomb* was the VMI cadet yearbook. He had a friend who had access to the five years he requested, sending him the five books on loan.

He had hoped to find a cadet picture of the young man who had been wearing the VMI shirt in one of them. He had a picture of the dead man's face, after it had been cleaned, and began searching through the yearbooks. It was amazing how many of the young men looked alike with the short-cropped hair and the military demeanor. If he wasn't there, he didn't know where he would search next.

John Starling had been invited again to have dinner with Curtis and his Aunt Dorothy in a couple days. It was Curtis who called and invited him, telling him it was at his aunt's suggestion. This time he took them up on it.

He was looking forward to telling Curtis the fort could stay on the land, but he wasn't going to tell him or his aunt he had bought it. He was especially looking forward to seeing Dorothy again. He still laughed to himself when he thought about Curtis calling her old. She was a beautiful woman. It had been a long time since he had dinner with a woman. Not since well before his divorce. In his heart, he still missed his wife, but he knew they would never be together again. It wasn't either of their faults. Still, it was time to move on.

John had one more thing to do before he got off. He looked around to make sure there would not be anyone who could overhear him. He called his friend Tommy McGill with the FBI.

Tommy answered the phone and was glad to hear from John. He told him he had been planning to call him to give the news about the voice mail he had received and the mention of *Operation Back Street*. Starling was just as surprised as Tommy was with the information.

He brought him up to date with everything he had to that point to include everything Gillam and Lovett told him about Lieutenant Jones and how they were afraid to take the information to their Internal Affairs Division or to the District Attorney with Jones having so many people in his pocket. Furthermore, they didn't want to blow the investigation into this *Operation Back Street* and its connection to all the strange deaths which had occurred. They were sure Jones had some connection to that as well.

Tommy agreed that the evidence they had was shaky at best and that one eyewitness against a police lieutenant was far from conclusive. He suggested that they all have a meeting soon and find out where they stood and if there was any other evidence or course of action they needed to take. He also had some information to share about *Operation Back Street,* but wanted to wait until he heard from his other source and hopefully from the person on the voice mail calling himself Grey Ghost.

Obviously, it was someone on the inside. Now there were two.

Gillam worked on the report while Lovett went and got the search warrant return signed by Judge Freeman and filed with the court. Gillam had this nagging feeling in the back of his head that there had been something recently on the news or in the papers regarding Judge Freeman, but he couldn't put his finger on it. He dismissed it for the time being and finished the report.

He did a background check on Tiny, aka Jamal Mathews. He had a record to include possession of marijuana, possession of a firearm, and theft by receiving a stolen auto. Now he had hit the big time. Trafficking in cocaine along with possession of a stolen handgun had him looking at anywhere between ten to twenty-five years if not more.

In addition, if Tiny sold the dope which was killing people, well, he might just get to meet 'Old Sparky.' The state's electric chair.

The other two people whom had been in the house were not residents and had been there to hang out with Tiny. The man had been found to have a violation of probation warrant out on him and the girl was found to have some weed in her pocket. They both were booked and were the guest of the Atlanta Pretrial Detention Center.

Larry wondered where the older woman whose bedroom

he had searched might be. The name on most of the papers found in the room was for an Edna Applegate. Records indicate the house and utilities were in the name of an Aaron Applegate. There was no criminal record for either name at that address.

Lovett returned to the office just as Gillam was finishing the reports and making copies for the files and one for Lieutenant Jones. He didn't make him a copy of the supplement which included the information about some of the cocaine being turned in to Mr. Hernandez at the State Crime Lab. He put it into a separate file in his desk.

There was one more thing Gillam wanted to do on this case. He wanted to go to the jail and see if Tiny had in fact wanted an attorney as the lieutenant had said. If he did, then fine, that would be it. But if he didn't then maybe he could persuade him to talk to him. It was worth the chance and an hour's worth of time.

General Cunningham was being briefed on the update of the internal investigation involving the missing batch of treated cocaine. The investigator, one of the general's own men, told him most of the cocaine had been recovered on the raid at the house belonging to their suspect, Cassandra Brown.

"Ms. Brown, a cleaning crew member, had stumbled across an unsecured test batch which was being refined and took it out in a garbage bag. The theft wasn't discovered for several hours. One of the hidden security cameras recorded her actions.

The background check on Ms. Brown failed to show anything questionable in her past because she used a deceased aunt's last name and social security number to get the job with the contract maintenance company. One of the analysts, a young lady, discovered the deception for us."

"Yes," the general interjected. "That's another reason we brought Ms. Jordon in on the team. So she could assist us with making sure everything was being checked now. She's one of those computer whiz kids who is smarter than anyone we have. Continue, captain."

"Once the theft had been discovered, it was found that Ms. Brown, or rather Ms. Mathews, as was her true name, was the most likely person to have taken it. It's believed she took the treated batch home and her son, Jamal Mathews, cooked it into crack and sold it out of the house. We conducted surveillance of the house and did the background on Jamal Mathews and turned the information over to Lieutenant Jones per your order for him to handle it on a local level as if it were just another crack house."

"And that was carried out in a timely fashion? What were the results?"

"Yes, sir. The Atlanta Police Narcotics Squad made several arrests during the raid where Lieutenant Jones took possession of the entire remaining product and made sure it had been turned over to one of our agents. The rest of what was believed to have been the entire stolen batch, was what had been sold out of the house and used by some of the locals. There may be a few residual reports of the product showing up, or rather reports of the strange overdoses, but there should be a sharp reduction immediately now that the product is off the street. Within a day or two I doubt there will be any more reports."

"And what about Ms. Brown, or rather, Ms. Mathews?"

"After the theft, she never returned to work. No one there has seen or heard from her. She didn't even pick up her last paycheck. We believe since she was not at the residence during the raid she may have gone into hiding before our surveillance started. We still have it in place in case she returns. We will attempt to get her whereabouts from her son. Once we have it, we will make sure we have all the product and there was no more distributed elsewhere. The total weight recovered is just short of what was taken by a few ounces and that may be attributed to what the victims had on them or smoked."

General Cunningham was interrupted by his phone and after a short conversation, excused the investigator if there was nothing further for him to report. When the investigator left, he continued the phone call for a short period. When it was completed, he buzzed one of his orderlies and told him to have King report to him first thing in the morning.

Gillam and Lovett drove over to the jail where they had Tiny brought out of a holding cell and into a conference room instead of one of the interrogation rooms. Somewhere they thought he might be more comfortable due to his size. Furthermore, it might make it a little less intimidating, hoping Tiny would be more inclined to talk.

Gillam read him his Miranda warnings from a small card he had in his billfold. Tiny told him he understood his rights. He said when he was brought out of the house he was put in a wagon and nobody said anything to him. They didn't even read him his rights just like he had done. He had not even talked with any lieutenant, but if a deal could be worked out, he was willing to talk.

"I'm not sure we can make a deal, Tiny," Gillam said. "You may be looking at murder charges."

"Murder, I didn't murder her. She had a stroke."

"Are you talking about Jessie?" Lovett asked.

"Jessie? I'm talking about mama. She was taking a bath at night and had a stroke. She had one of those, what do you call it, a hammerage. I found her the next morning.

"You mean a hemorrhage? What happened Tiny?"

"Oh, it was a mess. There was blood everywhere. It was even coming out of her eyes. I was going to call an ambulance, I really was, but she was already dead, and if they found out about it, I'd lose the house. I cleaned it up real good."

"If who found out about it?" Gillam asked.

"The bank people that own the house. They'd make me move." He looked down at the floor. "I don't have no place else to go. I thought I could stay there."

"So, where's Mama now, Tiny?"

"She's in the back yard." He looked up with a soft smile. "She always liked it back there."

Gillam and Lovett looked at each other. Lovett was almost afraid to ask, "Is there anyone else in the back yard?"

"No. We just didn't want no one to know."

"I'm sorry for your loss, Tiny," Gillam said. "But moving on, do you want to tell us about how you got the cocaine you were selling?"

"Are you going to charge me with murder?"

"I think your mama's death was the result of those bad drugs. I don't think you killed her at all."

"Sounds like it was an accident," Lovett added.

You could just see the pressure lift off the shoulders of the big guy. "Yeah, I'll tell you about those drugs. Those damn drugs. She told me everything when she brought them home. I wished she'd just left them where they were. Can I keep the house?"

After they had concluded at the jail, Gillam and Lovett went back to the office to finish the latest entry for the report. Another supplement which Gillam hid away in his desk. Gillam would call Doctor Higdon in the morning and tell him about the body in the backyard of Tiny's house.

He also called Detective Starling's number and left the information on his voice mail. In addition, he asked him to call his buddy at the FBI and tell him about the business where Tiny's mother worked and about the cocaine she took from one of the contract locations. He might be able to track it down faster than he could. Gillam wondered what connection Lieutenant Jones had with Tiny's mama and the drugs. Another piece of the puzzle.

They both decided it was time to call it a night and walked out to their cars. As they were leaving, Larry told Sam to say "hey" to Deb for him and in return, with a laugh, Sam said to do the same with Connie.

CHAPTER 25

Larry was almost home when he called his house and let the phone ring once, hung up and then called right back. This was the prearranged signal for Bubba to answer the phone. Bubba did and Larry told him he would be there in about fifteen minutes. Larry didn't want to suffer from any more headaches at the hands of Bubba. At least, headaches caused by blows to the head. There were plenty of other things, Bubba related, which caused Larry to have headaches.

When Larry got home, he unlocked and opened the door slowly, calling out that it was him. Bubba greeted him at the door with a smile.

"Welcome home, detective. Hope you had a good day." Something wasn't right. The house smelled clean, it looked clean, even Bubba was clean.

"Doris just left. She came over after work and helped me clean up today. She said it would go a long way in making you feel better about me staying here."

"Well, this is nice. Not what I expected to come home to at all. Thank Doris for me next time you see her."

"I will. There's some food in the fridge that we fixed for dinner. I saved you some. No rush, just whenever you're ready. It's just some meatloaf and mashed potatoes."

173

"That's good. I didn't get a chance to eat earlier. How about Cali? Did you feed her?"

"Oh, yes. She's great. We're getting along much better now."

"That's good. This is her house you know. She just lets me stay here too."

Gillam went into his bedroom and there was Cali laying on the bed licking at her paws. "Hey girl," he said, reaching over and stoking her side. She rolled over, grabbed his wrist with her front paws, and began licking his hand. "Yes, I missed you too." He got loose from her grasp and took off his holster, placing it on his dresser along with his badge and billfold. He took off his shoes and put on some moccasin type slippers. It was good to relax a little. He wished he could do it alone, but until they could get Bubba safely out into the open, he was stuck with him.

Before he went to eat anything, he thought if he was going to call Connie he had better do it before it got too late. He was nervous and tried to come up with some reason to put it off. There was no good reason to wait. He wanted to hear her voice. He stretched out on the bed next to Cali and called the number.

Connie answered and was delighted it was Larry. She told him she hoped he would call soon. He told her he was afraid it might be too late to call knowing she had to get up early, but she said she was just in bed reading. She liked to read for a while before going to sleep. It helped her relax.

She asked how his day had gone and he told her about the

raid they had been on, but didn't get into too much about all the crap with Jones. He did tell her Sam said "hey" and in turn, she told him to say "hey" back. He gave her just a little information to explain what had occurred at the stadium, but decided she didn't need to know all the details. Not yet anyway. Then he decided to take a chance.

"Connie, I don't want to rush it, but I'd like to see you again, soon if it's all right with you."

"That would be great," she said. "As long as it's not another ballgame. Not that I don't like them. I would just prefer something a little less crowded and maybe a bit less dangerous."

"I think I can manage that," he laughed. "There is something I want to say to you though. Something I've never said to another person."

"What would that be?" she asked, curiously.

"You see, I know God gave man his breath. However, in His wisdom, He must have given to a very few, select women, the ability to take that breath away. You have that ability because when I first saw you, that's exactly what you did to me."

"Oh, my!" She wasn't going to be able to fall asleep any time soon that night.

William N. Gilmore

CHAPTER 26

Doctor Higdon searched through all five copies of *The Bomb* every chance he had a free moment and couldn't be one-hundred percent sure, but he thought he might have found the young man's picture in one of them. There had been some which were close, so he got out his magnifying glass and looked them over several times. Yes. Yes, that had to be the one. Cadet Frank Morrison. Now to see if there was any more on this guy.

He hated to ask his friend to check on any confidential information for him since he didn't have access to it himself. He was sure there were some regulations and maybe even some laws which would be violated if they did. He had to ask. Otherwise, he was stuck again.

Near the end of her shift, while no one had been around her, Jenny sent The Magician the good news that the general had seemed interested in her eagerness to locate the intruder. He had been receptive about ordering some additional computer equipment.

She requested further instructions on how to proceed, but suggested that several dummy companies be set up with P.O. Boxes. She would give the general a list of those companies, as well as equipment for him to choose from, so it wouldn't look like she was steering him towards just one.

She also needed part numbers and order manifest, as well as prices which would be reasonable, but would not send up red flags. Everything needed to be real, or as close to real as possible, including the computer software and hardware. Something which would stand under scrutiny if anyone were to check. She was sure the general, not having a clear IT background, would have someone do just that.

She also sent him the other information he had requested although she wasn't real sure what he was up to at this point. He hadn't given her any further details on what else had been on his mind. She just had to be patient. That was not her strong point.

Azira had been waiting all day and all evening for a response from Jenny. He was relieved when it finally came. He slumped in his chair, finally able to relax for just a minute. Her suggestions were along the same lines he had been thinking. Great minds working together, separately. They could be implemented into his plan easily enough.

He was glad she was taking such a big hand in all of this as well. Furthermore, she sent the answers to several questions he had had and now it looked like there was some light at the end of the tunnel. He just hoped it wasn't a train bearing down on him.

There was a lot of work to do. It was late but there was

no time like the present to get started. He began an outline of what to do next. He would need the help of all his geek friends and if he were lucky, he would be able to meet Jenny face to face very soon.

William N. Gilmore

CHAPTER 27

Doctor Higdon was about to call Detective Gillam when he realized just how late it was. All the autopsies and tests being conducted made the time fly. He didn't even have a chance to have dinner. All the other assistants had been working just as hard and had pulled things together. There had only been two other deliveries of the same overdose situations in the past 12 hours and one additional report of one. Maybe it had reached its peak.

He would call Gillam and give him the information he had about the young man from the stadium in the morning, hoping soon to have more. In addition, test results conducted on the blood which was on the handkerchief used by Curtis to wipe his hands, showed results just like all the rest of the "overdosed" victims.

There was something embedded in the cocaine which caused massive destruction of the cells and blood vessels, but he was darned if knew what it was. It would take someone with many more degrees than he had and biological knowledge on the sub-atomic level which he probably didn't even know existed.

He was up to date on many things, but also, he was old school, and liked it that way. He hated all the new-fangled so-called science dealing with cloning and genetic engineering and the like. He felt like Man should just leave things well enough alone and stop playing God. On the other hand, maybe some of them are playing the other guy.

One other test which he made involved the bullet which had been recovered by Lovett from inside the ME's wagon. It was a 9mm, fully jacketed slug. The rifling, five lands with a right-handed twist, showed it most likely came from a Smith & Wesson semi-auto. Furthermore, it was Teflon-coated. Also known on the street as a 'cop killer', because it could go through a ballistic vest.

Gillam had just finished talking with Connie. They talked for quite a while. They both were looking forward to getting together again soon. Larry had been formulating a plan ever since he hung up. A picnic or a drive up to Helen for the day. Maybe even going over to Stone Mountain and doing the walking trails. He would have to think about it some more. He wasn't hungry or sleepy anymore.

He grabbed the journal belonging to Granger off the nightstand and began looking through that again. He couldn't believe all the corruption which was going on in the city and the county governments. He wondered if it was that way in all the big cities.

While reading over some of the entries, he came across a familiar name. Judge Judy Freeman.

It showed the judge receiving substantial 'loans' from an

un-named source to pay off gambling debts her son had acquired before they became public knowledge, embarrassing her and hurting her chances for re-election.

Her son had had visions of himself as somewhat of a playboy and a poker expert, but he had a problem with pills and alcohol which got him busted one night. Enter Lieutenant Jones to the rescue. He made it all go away. No report, no arrest record, no publicity. Now the judge was another on his list of those who owed him favors. From the entries in the journal, that list was substantial.

Larry was hoping Granger gave enough detailed entries that it was possible, the journal, along with Bubba's testimony, could be the smoking gun which would bring the lieutenant down. Gillam was almost scared to have too much hope. He was scared not to.

CHAPTER 28

Gillam pulled into the parking lot just as Sam did. They had both arrived well before the start of their shift. They didn't want to be late and give the lieutenant any ammunition to throw at them that early in the morning.

As they walked into the office, they saw Lieutenant Jones was already in his office with several people.

As Gillam and Lovett got to their desks, the men exited Jones' office and approached the detectives.

"Detective Lovett, I'm Lieutenant Decker with the Internal Affairs Division. I need to search your desk and locker."

"What's going on here?" Gillam asked, knowing somehow, they had been blindsided.

"You don't need to worry about it, Sergeant," Jones said. "Just back out of the way and let them do their job."

Lovett just stood there, dumbfounded at first. Finally, he said, "Okay, so what is this all about? My desk is open and you can search it anytime. I have nothing to hide. Is this a routine check or what?"

"We are investigating some missing evidence from a crime scene. Give Detective Anderson the keys to your locker and he'll check that out while I check your desk."

Lovett took out his keys, taking his locker key off the

William N. Gilmore

ring and handed it to the detective. "My desk is open. I have nothing to hide."

"No, it's not," returned Lieutenant Decker.

Sam reached over and pulled on the top drawer on his desk. It didn't open.

"I almost never lock this drawer. I know I didn't lock it last night when I left." He took out his key ring again, put the desk key into the lock, turned it, and opened the drawer slightly.

"Okay, you can stand back now," Decker said, putting on latex gloves.

Sam took a couple steps back, looked over at Larry and shrugged his shoulders.

Lieutenant Decker opened the drawer fully and removed an envelope from the drawer. On the envelope was written *Detective Sam Lovett*. Decker dumped the contents of the envelope on the desk. There were four small zip-locked bags and a metal tube crack pipe. The bags each contained a small hit of what appeared to be crack cocaine.

"That's not mine!" Lovett almost shouted. "That wasn't there yesterday."

"We're not saying it's yours, per se," Decker said. "At least, not at this moment. It's something you shouldn't have in your possession. It should have been turned in to property or to the Crime Lab. Right now, you're holding drug evidence improperly and it will continue to be under investigation. We'll check the envelope to see if there are any fingerprints on it."

186

"I'm being set up," Lovett swore, looking at the envelope, then straight at Jones.

"This is a bunch of crap," Gillam interjected. "All the drug evidence we've ever recovered *has* been turned in. There's no reason for Sam to have kept anything. He is not stealing or using drugs. Why don't you search my desk?"

"We already did. Yours was unlocked. You're in the clear for now. Unless it's found that you knew about Lovett holding onto evidence in violation of the SOP's."

The other IAD Detective returned and gave Lovett his locker key back telling Lieutenant Decker there was nothing, but some stained pants.

"Detective Lovett," Decker began, "until further notice, you are on administrative suspension. The chief will decide if it is to be paid or unpaid. A pending investigation by the IAD may determine if criminal charges will be forthcoming. Turn over your service weapon, badge, keys, and police identification to Lieutenant Jones. You will be escorted out. You cannot return until given permission. You will be allowed to make a statement later."

Sam reached for his weapon. For a split second, he wondered how many shots he could get off at Jones before they dropped him. As he grabbed his weapon, Jones' eyes widened with a sudden thought that Lovett might actually try something. Lovett slammed the weapon on his desk with a loud thud, causing several of the men to jump.

"The holster's mine," he said in disgust. He took off his badge, removed his identification from his billfold, took the office, desk and locker keys off his key ring, and tossed them on the desk as well.

Looking straight at Jones again, he asked, "Do you want my blood too, you murdering, low life, son of a bitch?"

Lieutenant Jones, horror flashing in his eyes for just a second, quickly tried to compose himself. "Get this little twerp out of here," he stammered. The color in his face had not returned following the shock of reality that the detectives somehow knew about Kim. It didn't go unnoticed by Gillam.

One of the IAD men started towards Lovett. And just as Lovett was about to head straight for Lieutenant Jones, Larry interceded and got between the men. "Get away from him. I'll take him." Taking hold of his arm and nudging him along, he said, "Come on Sam, let's not make things any worse. You need to get out of here. We'll work this out later."

Sam was hesitant, not wanting to move or take his eyes off Jones, but the constant pressure on his arm by Gillam directed him towards the exit. He gave one final look back and gave Jones a smile which did more than any words could.

Gillam got Lovett out of the building. He still had hold of Sam's arm, afraid he might turn and go back after Jones. He could feel the muscles tightening every time Sam clinched his fist.

"Look, Sam. I know those weren't yours, and you're being set up, but we must be careful what we say and how we do things. I think Jones knows now we have information he killed Kim. I could see it in him when you called him a 'murdering son of a bitch'."

"I'm sorry I let it slip. I just couldn't hold back. I think in a way, I wanted him to know. I want him to know it's me coming after him. I'm going to be the one to take him down. With your help, that is."

"I may be next," Gillam said. "It looks like he's trying to separate us and weaken our chances of going after him. It may not be as simple as a suspension. I think he's going to have to do something a little more desperate. We have big targets on our backs; more than ever now. We may have to go ahead and make a move sooner than we wanted."

William N. Gilmore

CHAPTER 29

Jenny was just leaving the general's office after getting approval for the order of the special router and software from one of the companies on the list she had made that morning, after getting the information from The Magician. She was to hand over the information to the floor supervisor who would have the order sent out. The items were to be shipped special one-day delivery, by a ground transportation company.

Captain King was sitting in the general's outer office, waiting to see the general that morning, as ordered. As Jenny was leaving, she looked over at King, smiled and wished him a good morning.

"Good morning to you, Ms. Jordan. You're looking lovely as ever."

"Thank you." She didn't care too much for the men there at The Facility, and especially those who were part of keeping her there. However, today she was in a good mood and high spirits. "I hope you have a great day," she said, as she kept waking back to her area.

"King," the general bellowed.

King went in and as was the casual custom, he did not report or salute. He just said, "Good morning, sir."

"Have a seat. There's something I want to go over with

you."

King sat at the chair in front of the general's desk. As he sat there, the general took out one of his cigars from the humidor sitting on his desk and cut the tip off.

It was then that King saw next to the humidor, a flashlight. It seemed out of place there at first and then it struck him. It was the flashlight from Morris's car. Why would the general have the flashlight?

"King, we may have a problem. I expect a good job performance. I expect obedience. I expect patriotism. Above everything else, I expect loyalty. If my people aren't loyal to me then everything I try to do is in constant conflict. I can't have my people working against me behind my back. I can't push a project through when my people are pushing from the other side. You get where I'm coming from?"

"Yes sir!" King said. But his eyes still flashed from time to time to the flashlight. The general put down the cigar and grabbed the flashlight. Kings eyes widened.

I have ordered men into battle. I knew, and they knew, they would not make it out. I have ordered men to sacrifice themselves for the sake of a few minutes of time or for a small scrap of dirt. These men went when ordered. They didn't ask why. They didn't cry or beg for it to be someone else. They didn't turn and run in the other direction. Now that's loyalty."

"Yes sir, but what has that got to do with right now. What kind of problem are you talking about?"

The general pointed the flashlight at King and pushed the button. King half expected to be blinded by the light in his eyes and turned his head slightly, but nothing happened. It didn't come on. The general reached into a drawer in his desk and pulled out a clear plastic bag. Inside the bag were two batteries and a key.

"Now Captain, what would your fingerprints be doing on these new batteries and a key, all of them in a flashlight which was in Morris' car?"

It didn't look like King's day was going to be that great.

William N. Gilmore

CHAPTER 30

Azira almost did a dance when the order came over one of the special dummy web sites he and his friends had set up. The order came from a local address, which made everything so much easier. Soon he would find out just where Jenny was being held.

The package was being delivered with a real router and software. One of his buddies suggested a tracker be put in the package as well. That idea was nixed just in case someone inspected the package before it got to Jenny. Something he was sure to happen.

After they found it was local, another idea they hoped to accomplish was for them to make the delivery themselves and to do surveillance. Just because an address had been given for the delivery did not mean that that was the final destination.

They wanted to make sure there was not a middle man prior to it going to Jenny. That's why they had also set up their own dummy delivery company used by the dummy computer equipment company. Hand in hand. These guys were smart; and fast. They had done all this last night and gotten the information to Jenny early this morning.

The delivery was to be made the next day at the address sent to them. A van could quickly be decked out to look like a delivery van. Azira wanted to be the one to make that delivery.

Now, Azira was making the arrangements for the next step of his plan. This had a lot more to do with physical work than it did computer work. Something he wasn't so used to. He needed to acquire some special equipment and hardware based on the information he had requested and received from Jenny. If this worked, it was going to be so cool. Stuff of which urban legends are made. If it didn't, well, he didn't want to go there.

Gillam told Sam he would call him later. He told him to go home and stay there. Keep his eyes open and think about what they could do to bring this situation to a close. Killing Jones was not an option at this point, he told him, knowing Sam's frame of mind right now. Besides, they had to prove Sam was innocent of any wrongdoing and they might need Jones alive to do that. But then again, maybe not.

Gillam watched Lovett drive away, then headed back to the office. He was going to find out just what Jones was up to and have it out with him. He got back and found Decker and his men had left and Jones was not in the office.

Gillam was thinking of taking several days off or maybe even a leave of absence. If he did that though, he might not have the access to the resources he needed. Furthermore, he might be able to keep a closer watch on Jones if he stayed on duty.

His phone was ringing on his desk and he was going to ignore it at first, but then thought it might be Sam calling him. It was Doctor Higdon. The doctor gave him a brief run down on the victim from the stadium, a former VMI cadet whose name was Morrison, as well as the test results on the handkerchief.

Unfortunately, there was still no word on what it was in the drugs which killed the victims. Larry in turn gave the doctor some of the info about what was going on there and again about Tiny's mother and her involvement. He also asked the doctor to contact Detective Starling and Agent McGill and pass all the information on to them. He apologized for putting more on him, but he just didn't have time to talk with everyone right now. Things were happening too fast.

"I'm sorry to hear that," the doctor said. "It sounds like there's a storm coming."

"The storms already here, doctor. Now it's time for the dam to burst and all hell to rain down."

After Lieutenant Decker and his men left, taking the evidence found in Lovett's desk with them, Jones, avoiding contact with anyone, also left, heading to his apartment.

Lovett had called him a murderer. That would mean his partner, Gillam, also knew. What information or evidence did they have? Why hadn't they come forward with it? Was it Kim, or did they know about his involvement with Granger? Or both? He needed to be sure before it went too far.

Jones pulled up in front of his apartment, looking around to make sure he hadn't been tailed. He went inside and locked the door behind him. He went into his bedroom and opened the drawer to the nightstand. He took out a blue, plastic box, opened it and there was his personal Smith & Wesson 9mm. He ejected the magazine and checked the ammunition. Fourteen fully jacketed, Teflon-coated, rounds in the mag and one seated in the chamber.

He had cleaned it well and oiled it after its last use. He was already wearing his duty weapon in its holster on his right side, so he put the weapon inside his waistband at the small of his back.

He had made a good shot with it. If only Kim hadn't been so damn stubborn and had co-operated when he got him to meet with him.

He tried to get Kim to release the body to him. Lied to him saying he would be taking the body to a government facility for a special investigation. Gave him part of the truth telling him it was a government cover-up and he was part of an undercover sting operation. Kim would have none of it.

Jones had had his personal weapon with him and used it as Kim began to drive away. He was glad he didn't have to get rid of it after seeing the bullets exit wound. It was his favorite.

He was sure the bullet would never be recovered and if by some chance, it was, he was also sure it could never be traced back to him. Now he may have to put it to use again. That would suit him just fine. He had two targets in mind. Seven bullets apiece and they could flip for the last one. That made him laugh.

For just a second, anyway.

He went to his closet and took out a small, metal lock box. Inside was a passport and other papers. He took a suitcase out of the closet as well and packed it with some of his clothes and items needed for a fast get-away just in case. In the closet, under the carpet, was a cover over a hole.

He removed the cover, reached down into the hole and took out a bag, which was in fact a large, white sock. Inside the sock was cash. Over $20,000 in one-hundred dollar bills. That was just the beer money. The real stash was in a safety deposit box at a local bank. Part of that stash included his little black book of names and things which people wanted kept quiet. Things they reluctantly paid to keep quiet or things they could do for Jones when the time was right. It was just about that time to put it to its best use.

Gillam had gone to his own apartment. After calling Bubba and alerting him, he went inside and grabbed Granger's journal. He didn't have time to explain to Bubba what was going on. He was on a mission.

He thought a preemptive strike was in order. He thought about calling Sam, but it might be best not to get him any more involved right now. He was already up to his neck in trouble and besides, if things didn't work out, he might need Sam to rescue him later. It wasn't about a dam breaking anymore. He was afraid the whole damn world might cave in.

William N. Gilmore

CHAPTER 31

King was stuck in a difficult situation. Now he wished he had not come back. The general was waiting for an answer. He didn't have one.

"Well, Captain. Have you had enough time to come up with something?"

"General, you talk about loyalty," King began. You know I've been loyal. I've busted my butt for you. I've even taken out one of your 'loose ends' for you."

The general's eyes narrowed at King.

"Was that what you had in store for me? Was I one of your 'loose ends' general?"

"You were my right hand. You were a part of everything. What makes you think I want you gone? Did you see the note I gave Morris? It was for Morris to take out that Granger fellow and then at the right time, that stupid police lieutenant and those nosey detectives of his."

"Then why did he have pictures of *me*? Why had I been followed? Didn't you trust me? Where was your loyalty to me?"

"That was something he must have done on his own after I told him I was going to put the two of you together. I wanted you to get more field experience. Learn from him. I wanted you to have a more hands on position. I was moving you up. That is, until he was compromised and he needed to be reassigned."

King stared at the general, not knowing what to believe right then.

"Then there was the incident at the stadium. Now I have to bring someone new in. I still want you to get all the experience and training I can provide for you here. But I can't have you thinking I'm trying to have you removed and I can't have you lying to me. There's too much at stake now. The final testing stages are set to begin very shortly. The lab says we are getting close to having a product which can be mass produced and distributed within several weeks."

"Yes sir, I saw the note Morris had and I knew it came from you. I thought you had turned your back on me and I was trying to make sure I wasn't a target for elimination. I was scared and after you found out I took out Morris, I thought for sure you would suspect I was turning on you, but I wasn't. I did it to protect you. You and the mission."

"Now see. That's what I'm talking about when I say I demand loyalty. You went beyond your normal scope. You took that extra step to keep the mission safe. I just wanted to hear you say it. Is there anything else I need to know? Any other problems or reservations?"

"No, sir. Nothing right now."

"Good. I want you to keep close tabs on that police lieutenant. He could cause problems if he goes rogue on us and starts doing things on his own again. If he does, you know what needs to be done. Those two detectives of his are still snooping around as well. Make sure they don't find anything. I'll get you some men to help. That's all."

"Thank you, sir." King got up and left the office. He felt better now knowing the general was behind him after all.

The general buzzed his orderly and told him to have Richards report to him. He was disappointed King didn't tell him about the call he had made to the FBI. He might have been able to explain it away, but keeping it a secret; that was another lie. It didn't matter what truths were told. It was the spoken and unspoken lies that mattered. He just wasn't going to put up with disloyal people under his command. No matter who it was.

Azira and a couple of his friends had fixed up a van to look just like a delivery van to include painting on logos and DOT numbers. They hoped everything would come off the rented van when it was time to turn it back in. They even put empty boxes in the back and had set up a video camera in the grill. A uniform was put together as well.

A team had already done a drive by of the address and stated it looked like a one-story warehouse with a fence around it. There was a working smokestack. They most likely have an incinerator.

Photographs and a satellite image didn't show much more. There was a gatehouse with a guard at the entrance. A ramp going to an underground entrance may have been an underground parking garage. There were some regular doors and a couple roll up doors that were visible. Several surveillance cameras could be seen positioned around the building and one at the gatehouse.

Azira was getting a good feeling that this was the place where Jenny was located. It had all the earmarks of a nondescript, commercial warehouse except there was no work going on. No workers besides the guard were visible. No trucks loading or coming in or out. There was too little activity outside for a business of that type. Everything must be going on inside behind closed doors and out of sight. A covert government facility for sure.

Azira, sitting in the driver's seat of the van, nervous as hell, but excited too, went over his lines several times. The package, addressed to a Ms. Pettigrew, c/o Black Bird Distributors, sat in the passenger seat. He had a clipboard fixed up with a manifest of several bogus deliveries he had already made and several more to make after this one.

He was ready to go. The surveillance team was already in position. If there was trouble, he would try to get out with the van, but if he couldn't, a car was waiting to rush in and pick him up. That is, if he made it outside the gate. No one was going to go up against an armed security officer.

He took a deep breath and gave a wave as he headed out. The rest of the team had radios and let everyone know that The Magician was on his way.

The video camera showed the van approaching the gate and the security guard coming out and holding up his hand.

Azira stopped at the gatehouse and told the guard he was with Magic Man Package Delivery Service. He showed the guard the invoice and the package and he was directed to one of the front entrances after the guard took his name and license tag number.

So far, so good. He had almost been afraid he was going to have to leave the package with the guard. That would not be good. He drove up to the building and went to the entrance door where he encountered a speaker box. He pushed the button and looked into a camera.

"Yes?" A crackling, disembodied voice said.

"Magic Man Delivery Service with a package for a Ms. Pettigrew."

He heard a buzzer and opened the door. He entered an office which you might find in any warehouse. There were all kinds of papers on bulletin boards, a time clock with a rack of time cards and two cluttered desks with papers, pictures, and coffee cups. There was a single door at the other end of the office. An older woman sat at one of the desks and using her finger, called him over.

"Where do I sign?"

"Are you Ms. Pettigrew?"

"I'm authorized to sign for her."

"No ma'am. We have strict rules when it comes to these

delicate computer parts. I have to have Ms. Pettigrew sign for it. You don't want me to lose my job, do you?"

The woman, gave him a blank stare, picked up her phone, and punched a couple numbers.

"She'll be right here."

"Is it going to take long? I really have to go to the bathroom. Do you have a bathroom I can use?"

"It will be just a minute. We don't have one for the public. Sorry."

"Then I'll have to leave and come back later. I can't wait. I have to go now!" He headed for the exit.

"Hold on just a moment there," the woman said, with some disdain. She got back on her phone and in a second, a man came through the door and told Azira to follow him.

He was led down a brightly lit hallway with several doors. At the end of the hallway, they went through another door. They entered a larger section which took them to what appeared to be a break room. There were a few people in the break room. Several were wearing white lab coats. One was wearing a military uniform. He was directed across from that and there were the restrooms.

Azira entered the restroom alone and seeing no one else there, he went into a stall. He took a deep breath. He had made it this far. He waited a short time, flushed the toilet and exited the restroom.

Seeing his escort had gone into the break room and was

talking with one of the men in a lab coat, he turned the opposite way he had come in, went to a door and opened it. He was just about to go through when his escort called to him "This way, son. That's off limits."

Azira was escorted back to the front office where Ms. Pettigrew was waiting on him and showed him an ID badge.

"Sorry about that, but you know when it's time to go …,"
He handed her the clipboard and showed her where to sign. He handed her the package. He turned to the woman at the desk and said, "Thank you, so much." Again, he got a blank stare.

He headed out the exit and to his van. When leaving, he had to stop again at the gatehouse. The guard signed him out and then waved him on through. Piece of cake.

Jenny received an open box from her floor supervisor, Ms. Pettigrew. The box contained a computer router and an instruction CD which included software for the router.

Jenny almost laughed out loud when she saw the delivery company's name on the invoice that was left in the box. Magic Man. He sure was. She made the entry to let him know she had received the package. She was about to find out just where she was. The first step in getting her out of there.

William N. Gilmore

CHAPTER 32

Lieutenant Jones was calling to use some of the leverage he had on one of the names in his black book. He was going to need help dodging any allegations Gillam and Lovett might throw at him. He needed to make sure he had someone on his side who had the power to make everything disappear. He was calling Judge Freeman.

He had had her on a short leash for such a long time and now it was time for her to prove her worth. He might even think about letting her off that leash if she were able to pull this off. Nah, she was too valuable to him.

Judge Freeman answered the call from Jones on her private line. He explained there were some people trying to set him up and she might hear things about him, but they were not true. He said he needed to get arrest warrants for two detectives who had stolen drugs and had been involved with the cover-up and possibly the commission of a murder. Maybe two.

"I can be there in a couple hours, Judge, after I have the warrants typed up."

"I'm afraid I have a previous engagement I can't break. Would first thing tomorrow morning be soon enough?"

He said he would be there around 8 a.m. if that was

convenient.

She agreed and would be in her chambers waiting on him. He hung up with the judge and headed back to his office to write up the arrest warrants. He couldn't help but smile.

Jones only wanted the warrants so he could go after Gillam and Lovett on the pretense of trying to bring them to justice. Two good cops gone bad and now involved with murder, drugs, and who knows what other corrupt activities. Sweet.

The newspapers and the television stations would eat it up. Maybe even make him a hero. Too bad Gillam and Lovett wouldn't survive the arrest, he thought, and maybe, just maybe, he would come out of this squeaky clean. Now *that* would impress those other guys.

Judge Freeman hung up the phone. "Was that good enough for you, detective?"

"Perfect," Gillam said. He was standing next to the judge having listened in on the conversation. "I'm sorry you got so mixed up with him," tapping Granger's own little black book. "He's poison. But maybe this will go a long way to rectify some of what he had done to you and many others."

"I hope so," she said. Her voice cracking just a bit along with a sniffle. She called out to her legal assistant, "Have Judge Hildebrand come in, please."

Judge Hildebrand, an older man with white hair and a white beard, reminding Gillam of the Santa Claus in the original

Miracle on 34th Street, came into Judge Freeman's chambers.

"Judge Hildebrand, this is Detective Gillam. He has a story to tell you. I can confirm some of the information he is about to give you, but then I'm afraid I must recuse myself from any further proceedings dealing with this matter. The reasons will come out shortly."

"Judge," Gillam started, pointing over to a chair. "This is Bubba Thompson."

Sam hadn't heard from Larry in some time. He wasn't answering his cell phone, home phone, or the office phone. He was starting to get antsy and felt like he had to do something.

Debbie was home now and he had told her everything which had happened at the office. She wanted him to stay home, but knew he had to go and check on Larry. She needed to know too. Sam went into his closet, to the very back and pulled open the door to the hidden compartment. Inside were many handguns hanging on pegs.

He first grabbed a Colt .357 Python, but then, put it back and took down a Sig Sauer P-229, .40 caliber semi-automatic. It held thirteen hollow-point rounds including one in the chamber. He may need the extra ammo it held. He grabbed a couple more magazines and loaded them up.

He grabbed a small gym bag, put the weapon and the extra mags in it, and then decided to take the Colt anyway along with a box of shells. Debbie was looking in her closet as well, which had the same configuration.

"Just what do you think you're doing there, missy?" Sam was standing with his hand on his hips.

"I'm not going unarmed."

"You're not going at all."

"And why not?"

"I need you to stay here, baby. All hell is going to break loose and I may not be able to keep you safe. If I'm trying to do that, then I won't be able to keep me safe. Understand?"

"Yes," she said, reluctantly. A little crack in her voice. "You better bring your sorry ass right back through that door the same way it goes out. No holes and no parts missing. Especially the good parts." She crossed the floor and threw her arms around his neck.

"Every part is a good part to me," he said, squeezing her to him. "Don't worry, I will. And I'll bring that no good partner of mine back as well. I think he's starting to grow on me. Besides, the future Mrs. Connie Gillam may want him back in one piece too."

CHAPTER 33

He knew it. He just knew that was the place. Azira had been right. Jenny got the package just shortly after he delivered it at the warehouse. The surveillance team said there had been no traffic in or out of the gate before he got the computer message. There was no other conclusion. That was it.

He hadn't been able to see much inside the warehouse, but what he did see gave him ideas about what might be going on. When he opened the restricted area door outside of the restrooms, he saw a corridor with rooms on either side with large windows facing the corridor. Inside the rooms were what appeared to be lab stations. He saw people inside those rooms wearing surgical masks, gloves, and hair coverings. Just like in an operating room. He also saw a lot of various test tubes, beakers, and medical type equipment.

There was one other thing he saw which bothered him more than the rest. He saw cages. In one room, he saw some with dogs, some empty. In another, he saw small monkeys and chimpanzees. Obviously, these were animals used for experiments. He had seen all this in just an instant. It had taken all his reserve to keep from showing any disgust. Maybe it was all legal, but it just wasn't right. Now he knew what the incinerator was being used for.

Lovett drove straight to Larry's apartment. He had tried several times to reach him at all his numbers, but without success. When he arrived at the apartment, he didn't see Larry's car. He didn't see Doris' either. He went to the door and standing to one side, he tried the doorknob. It was locked. He knocked on the door and yelled in. "Bubba, it's Sam, Sam Lovett, Larry's partner. There was no answer. He tried one more time, but again there was no response.

He took his keys out and found the key Larry had given him just in case of emergencies, or if he needed Sam to feed Cali. He unlocked the door and pushed it open half-expecting Bubba to be standing there with his favorite tire iron. There was nothing. He called in and only heard his own voice. He went in, hugging the wall and inching forward. There was nothing there.

He checked the living room, the kitchen, and he got to Gillam's bedroom where the door was half-open. He pushed it open and came around the corner to draw down on Cali, lying on the bed. She meowed at him and continued to lick her paws. No one else was there. No Gillam, no Doris, not even Bubba.

Thankfully, there also was no blood or any other signs of anything out of the ordinary, but there also was no note or any indication where they had gone or if they were together.

He called the police dispatchers line and got hold of Doris. She hadn't picked up Bubba and she didn't know where he was. She hadn't heard Gillam on the radio either. He asked her to patch him over to Simmons. He heard a humph from her and then Simmons answered.

"Simmons, this is Lovett. Do you still have that information on the GPS in Gillam's detective car?"

"Yeah. I couldn't find out who put it there, but I did give Gillam a GPS signal blocker to use whenever he was out in it. All you have to do is plug it into your cigarette lighter. You can pick one up at any spy shop or on-line."

"Great! If he's not using it, is there any way you could find out where the car is now?"

"Sure. I was able to get the frequency using a radio transceiver. It's somewhere in the 900 MHz range, I recall. I have it written down here somewhere. But you need to be within a few blocks of it to get a good signal on the tracker. There's so many out there.

"That's not good," Lovett said. "I don't even know where to start looking. He could be anywhere. Do me a favor. Keep monitoring the radio and if you hear him or get any reports at all about, well, you know, any incidents that may be him, call me."

"I'll do that. Be careful out there."

Sam left the apartment, leaving Cali in charge after making sure she had food and water, not knowing when Larry would return. He locked the door behind him.

He wasn't sure where to look. He didn't think he was at the office and it probably wouldn't be a good idea to go there looking for him. He didn't think he would be at Connie's. Not with Bubba in tow. Maybe the ME's office? He called there first.

No need making a trip for nothing and he was right. No one had seen or heard from him since earlier today. Doctor Higdon told him about some of the conversation he and Gillam had had. He told him that Larry sounded as if everything was coming to a head. That didn't sound good. He knew that Larry wanted Jones just as bad as he did. Well, almost.

CHAPTER 34

Azira knew time would now be a factor. He immediately sent the next set of instructions to Jenny. These made even less sense to her than the previous ones, but apparently, The Magician knew what he was doing. She hoped so anyway. So did Azira.

While Azira had been busy delivering the package to the warehouse, another group of brainiacs got the second phase of what was being termed, *The Rescue,* up to full speed. They were using a mechanic's garage to get everything ready. They needed the blowtorches and heavy machines to get most of the work done.

This had been no small operation. The speed at which everything was getting accomplished astounded Azira. He was thrilled though. The word had gone out on an underground network for help in equipment and supplies. It was amazing how many people showed up and wanted to contribute. Azira had a lot of friends who had friends, and that in turn spilled over to a lot of resources to make things work. Without everyone's help, he knew this would not happen.

People contributed their expertise, their time, and even some, their cash. An old, blue, coffee can, which once held nails and screws, now had a sign on it, which simply read, *Free*

Wonder Woman Fund. It was almost full. The money would go to help pay for the rented van, the computer equipment, food and snacks for everyone, and the machine.

Jenny waited in the break room until she was alone. She would only have a few minutes. She went over to the Coke machine and with all her strength, she was able to pull it out a bit from the wall. She unplugged it from the wall and then using a pair of scissors she had hidden in in her pocket, she began trying to cut the thick electoral cord as close to the machine as possible. She prayed no one would walk in on her.

It took several times of her squeezing the scissors with both hands before she could cut through. She plugged the male part back into the wall and let the rest of the cut cord hang behind the machine. Then she forced it back towards the wall where it had been.

She was out of breath and her hands were sore. She took out the typed sticker she had made and put it over the one already on the machine. She taped it to the machine with tape she had wrapped around one finger. Just as she finished, a group of people walked into the break room. She hit the machine and began to swear.

"Stupid thing is out of order again," she said loudly, directing her frustration to the people as they sat at a table. "It's a piece of crap. When are they going to replace this thing?"

"Maybe you should tell a supervisor," one of the group

suggested.

"Yeah, right. As if that would do any good. It only matters to them when they want to use it."

"Maybe if you tell them how much it would mean to you or that there have been many other complaints."

"Oh, I've made lots of complaints. They all fall on deaf ears."

"Maybe you need tell them a little louder."

"You're right. I think I'll do that right now."

Jenny made a big production of storming out of the break room. When she was out, she did go to her supervisor, Mrs. Pettigrew.

"That stupid Coke machine is out of order again and the cafeteria is closed. Can't you get someone to fix that thing or at least bring us a new one?"

"I'll have someone look at it later and see what needs to be done. It might just have a jam or something."

"You know, I don't have much here. I can't go out to the nearest McDonalds. I can't even go out for pizza. I can't go to the movies with my friends or even go to a club. All I have is that stupid break room right now and those stupid machines, and you don't even care if I have those. All you want me to do is—"

"All right, Ms. Jordan, all right. I'll go see what needs to be done with it right now. If it's broken, we'll get it fixed or replaced. You just need to settle down. You don't want to get yourself in any trouble by making a scene."

"I'm sorry," she said, more restrained. "Thank you. Yes, please check it now. I think I'm having caffeine withdrawals. I don't like coffee and I need a soda, soon."

"Okay! I'm on my way right now." *Anything to keep your yippy little mouth shut and get you back to work*, she was thinking.

Mrs. Pettigrew went to the break room and tried to get the Coke machine to work. She didn't know anything about its internal operations, it just didn't work. There were no lights on and no noise came from it. She looked behind the machine as far as she could get and saw it was plugged in. She hit it several times and still it didn't work. Some people in the break room told her it was broken. She looked on the front of the machine and saw a distributors name and repair number. She wrote the number down, went to her office, and called to get the machine repaired or replaced as soon as possible. When she called, she was delighted to get a very nice and helpful young man who apologized for all the problems with the machine and he promised if he couldn't get a crew to fix it, he would personally have a new one delivered. In fact, to save time, he would have the repair crew bring one with them. She also wanted to have them come first thing in the morning before the first shift started. He said it would be no problem. *It was so nice to have quick, friendly service*, she thought.

CHAPTER 35

Doctor Higdon called Detective Starling's office, but he was not in. Next, he called Tommy McGill and gave him all the information which Gillam had forwarded.

"So," Tommy replied, "you be telling me that this woman who worked for some bloody cleaning company, stole the drugs from this place and those are the same drugs that are responsible for all those deaths?"

"That's what it appears."

"And this place where the drugs came from, what is it? A business of some kind?"

"We didn't get that information. We just know it was the last place she went with the cleaning crew. We're not even sure which day it was. We were hoping you might be able to get the information for us quicker than we could with Gillam busy and Lovett out of commission. Maybe even find out what this business is and where it is."

"Okay, I tell you what I can do. I'll call her company and see if I can get the address of the last place she went with the cleaning crew. I'll get with my lads and see if they can come up with something as well. I'll get back to you when I do. As for Lieutenant Jones and the detectives, I'm not sure what I can do right now. It sounds like an internal matter there at the department. They have to come up with something more before our agency can step in on that. But if we can tie him in with everything else that's going on, we may have a racketeering charge which would bleed over to the federal level."

"Thanks for your help there, Agent McGill. I'll pass it on."

Tommy got the information about Cassandra Brown's employment and assignment history after faxing over a subpoena to the Bright Spot agency and talking with a manager. Now he needed information about that last location she had been assigned. He got Azira on his cell. He could barely hear him for all the background noise on Azira's end.

"What are you doing? It sounds like you're in a bloody construction zone."

"Something like that," Azira said as he walked out of the garage and around the side of the building. With most of the noise abated, he told Tommy he was on a special project.

"I've got something I need checked out as soon as possible. I need to see what kind of activity is going on at a place called, Black Bird Distributors."

"What? What did you say?"

"Get away from all that noise. I said Black Bird Distributors. See what kind of company it is, what their background is, and who's running the bloody thing."

"Why? What have you heard?"

"It may be a front for a clandestine drug operation. It's possible that's where some bad drugs came from that got out on the street and are killing people."

"Tommy, that's where Jenny is."

"Jenny? You're *Wonder Woman,* Jenny? How do you know that? Are you sure?"

"I've been there. I didn't see her myself, but I've confirmed she's there."

The cat was out of the bag now. He went ahead and told Tommy some of what had transpired so far. Tommy wasn't very happy with him. He didn't tell him about the rescue which was about to be launched. What he did say though, was a mouth full.

"Black Bird Distributors," Azira continued. "That's *Operation Back Street.*"

"Listen to me," Tommy said sternly. "I don't want you doing anything further until you hear back from me. Is that clear?"

"I hear you." Azira had no intention of cancelling his plans to get Jenny out of there. Especially now that it appeared she may be in more danger than he had first thought.

"Don't go near that bloody place. I'll call you in a bit."

"I won't," Azira lied.

Tommy called John Starling's cell phone. He told him Doctor Higdon had attempted to reach him and then told him about Black Bird Distributors, although there were still questions in his mind whether this was a real government operation.

"You need to call Detective Gillam," Starling told him. "He needs to know everything that's going on as well. He might have some more input by now." He gave him Gillam's cell phone number as well as Lovett's.

Starling called the ME's office and talked with Doctor Higdon. After trading information about the *Operation Back Street* and the Black Bird Distributors connection, they arranged for Starling to meet with Jaccob at the house where the body of Cassandra Brown was believed to be buried in the back yard. The body was to be exhumed and taken back to the ME's office for examination to see if Tiny's story was accurate.

Tommy tried to call Detective Gillam, but there was no answer. He left a voice mail to call him as soon as possible. He next tried Detective Lovett's cell and thankfully, got him.

"I need to get with you and Gillam about this *Operation Back Street*."

"I've been put on suspension and Gillam is out there somewhere and he may be with our witness. I can't get hold of him and I don't know where he is. Lieutenant Jones knows we know about his connection with Kim's death and he may now be on the run or after Gillam. I'm running around like a chicken with its head cut off and I don't know where to look anymore."

"I heard about the suspension and Jones' involvement,

but I can't help you with that right now. I do need to know something though. The owner of the house where you did the raid and recovered the cocaine, that was Cassandra Brown, right?"

"Yeah, that's right. But her real last name was Mathews. Why?"

"She's the one who took the cocaine while working for a cleaning outfit. She took it from a business they had a contract with known as Black Bird Distributors."

"Okay, keep going." Sam was trying to figure out where he was going with this.

"The car and van which followed you, that was part of what we now know to be *Operation Back Street*. What we believe to be some secret government project."

"Okay," Sam interjected. "Now you're going off in two different directions."

"No. Because they're one in the same."

"What? What makes you think that?"

"I've had someone inside the bloody place for a while and didn't even know it until recently."

"You have an undercover agent inside *Operation Back Street*?"

"Well, not exactly. It's a young lass that's been in contact with my techno-friend. She's being kept there under false pretenses. Almost like blackmail. She's doing some computer work there for them."

"But you're the FBI, for God's sake. That's kidnapping. Can't you do something about that? Can't you go in there and get her and find out what's really going on there?"

"I think it's over my head. According to another source, the military is involved. There's a General Cunningham who's running the show. I just found out that *Operation Back Street's* cover and base is this Black Bird Distributors, a warehouse type building, not far from downtown. I have an address now and a partial layout. They have labs there as well. That may be where the cocaine is being manufactured or altered."

"If it's government run and controlled, what can we do? Who do we call about something like that? Why would they have cocaine there in the first place?"

"I'm not sure. And what did they do to the cocaine for it to act so horribly on people? Wasn't it bad enough already? I don't trust anyone outside our own little circle now."

"Oh, my God. I wonder if that's what Lieutenant Jones has been doing. Cleaning up some of the mess which came from one cleaning lady stealing some bad coke. I bet they didn't see that coming. I don't know how he got involved, but Jones must have been trying to keep the bodies and evidence from being processed. He killed Kim in order to take the body of the homeless guy, and I bet he tried to torch his office with that gas bomb after taking Jessie's body. I have to get hold of Gillam. He needs to know all this right now. Jones, the snake that he is, may be ready to strike at any moment. If only I knew where either one of them were."

"If I had any more evidence against Jones, I'd put out a city-wide APB on him. I just don't have enough. Maybe if we were to find Gillam and his witness in time, we could—"

"What do you mean 'in time'? Don't start that stuff. He's out there with a killer that's got a badge and nothing to lose now. Jones has some friends in high places or at least some people that are scared to say no to him. All Gillam probably has is a 350-pound anchor and a target between his eyes. We need to find him first. We have to."

Leaving the courthouse, Gillam headed back to his car with Bubba following. He grabbed his cell phone and tried to call Sam. His phone was dead. He had forgotten to charge it. He couldn't even check to see if he had any messages. Did he leave the charger in the car or was it in his apartment? No, it was at the office. He had taken it out to plug in Simmons' GPS blocker. He had so much on his mind he just plain forgot about it. That was the last time he'd ever do that. At least, until the next time.

The fact that Bubba's resurrection was about to become public, made it even more important to keep him hidden in a location unknown to anyone. Larry took Bubba to a local hotel.

It wasn't one of the fanciest or most expensive ones, but it wasn't a dump either. He wanted to make sure it didn't have a lot of seedy characters around that would sell information for a few dollars or a bag of drugs. Somewhere Bubba could be out of sight and not get into trouble. He paid for the two-bed room in cash and took both key cards. He made sure there would be no disturbances. No maid service, no phone calls, in or out, and definitely, no room service. There wouldn't be any visits by Doris.

He didn't call Lovett from the hotel just in case there were some traces being made on their phones now. He was going to be really careful. He told Bubba he would be back for him in a while after he took care of some business. Bubba gave a frown. He said he would bring him back something to eat. That made Bubba smile.

Gillam stopped in at a Super Wall-Mart he had passed earlier and bought a new disposable cell phone. He also bought a hat and had thoughts about buying a wig, but that was going overboard. He grabbed some fried chicken from the deli along with some potato salad. He got enough for three. He might just join Bubba. He took their pre-packaged forks and knives and some paper plates as well.

He headed back to the hotel while the meal was still hot and when he got there, he found Bubba asleep on one of the beds. He almost hated to wake him, but the snoring demanded it. He gave him the package of chicken and potato salad.

Bubba asked, "What did you get for yourself to eat?"

"That's not all for you. We're sharing."

"What did you get for us to drink?" Bubba said, looking

into the sack.

"There are cups in the bathroom and a thing they call a faucet. Turn the knob on that faucet thing and believe it or not, water comes out of that middle thing. Isn't that amazing? You can even drink it. What will they come up with next?"

"I like to have a soda or two when I eat."

Gillam walked over to Bubba and grabbed the sack of chicken away from him.

"Well then, I guess you won't be wanting this without your precious sodas," Larry said, almost throwing the sack across the room.

"Wait!" Bubba said, reaching out with both hands, but still several feet short of being able to rescue the bag. His eyes wide in the seeming fear of losing the smallest morsel of food. However, the softest, childlike voice came out of the big man.

"I'm sorry," he said, putting his arms down. "That was rude of me." He had lowered his head as well. "Water is fine. Thank you for getting the chicken for us. I like potato salad too." You could tell in his voice he was being sincere.

"I'm sorry too. I over-reacted." Gillam tossed the bag over to Bubba. "Eat all you want. I need to charge up this cell phone." He grabbed the store bag, removed the pre-paid cell phone package, and opened it. He plugged the socket into the wall plug. "This should only take a little while. Then maybe we can find out what's going on out there."

Bubba took some of the chicken out and put it on a plate

along with a good helping of the potato salad. He took it over to Gillam as he sat on the bed. "It's been a rough week for everyone. Let's eat."

CHAPTER 36

King felt a little better after his meeting with the general. His years of seeing things change in a heartbeat, hidden agendas, and outright lies kept him from being too comfortable. He would continue to do his duty as was expected of him, but he would keep his eyes open and watch his back.

He thought about the call he had made to the FBI. Maybe it wasn't the smartest move he ever made, but it was an option he wasn't ready to dismiss. It was always good to have backup plans.

King received information that Lieutenant Jones was acting suspiciously. The surveillance team, with the additional men the general had assigned, said the lieutenant had packed a bag and taken it with him. He then went to a bank where he was known to have a safety deposit box, but there were no attempts to leave the city. He had gone back to his office and was still there.

It looked like Lieutenant Jones might be getting ready very soon to break away from everything. His usefulness had just about come to an end. King thought Jones might need to disappear. For good. It was almost ironic. Someone was thinking the exact same thing about King.

Azira had almost everything ready. Nearly all the work had been completed. There were just a few touch ups and some extra equipment to get ready. He had a truck that had been borrowed and it would be loaded soon. It sat in the garage ready to roll at the right moment. Azira wanted to go with it, but that would put things at risk. He had already been seen in The Facility. He would be close though. Nothing could keep him away.

He made sure the two guys going with the truck looked the part and had all the information they needed. He sent some final instructions to Jenny. These would be simple. He hoped they would be. He waited patiently for the response. There was too much that could go wrong. He hoped God, karma, the stars, luck, and everything else he could think of was on their side. They were too close for it to get screwed up now. But not quite close enough.

Jenny received the instructions and understood her part. She knew it was a risk. She also knew if she did get out of The Facility she may have all kinds of people looking for her. The police, maybe even the FBI, or possibly a hit man. And if they found her, then what? Back to jail, turned back over to the general, or even worse, disappear forever. She might have to go into hiding for years. Anything was better than being stuck at The Facility. Doing things for them that might be bad. She didn't want that on her conscience any more.

Just then, Mrs. Pettigrew came over to her and told her the general wanted to see her. Now.

Jenny started to shake a little and took the trek to the general's office.

"Ms. Jordan, you received the computer equipment you requested. How soon will I get that hacker?"

"Give me two days General and I'll have my hands on him before he can say 'How do you do'."

"I'll hold you to that, Ms. Jordan."

Jenny left the general's office and went back to her workspace. Mrs. Pettigrew came by again and Jenny motioned her over. Mrs. Pettigrew asked her if everything was all right.

"I'm not feeling too good right now. I think I'm going to be sick."

After Gillam and Bubba had eaten their chicken, Gillam found the cell phone had a sufficient charge to make some calls. His first call was to Lovett.

"Where the hell have you been?" Sam demanded, with more concern than anger. "Is Bubba with you? Are you all right?"

"Yes, Bubba's with me and we're both okay. My phone died and I thought it might be better if I got a disposable to use just in case I could be traced. I even used that GPS blocker Simmons gave me."

"Where are you?"

"I'd rather not say right now. Big brother and all. Are you okay?"

"Just worried out of my gourd that you might be somewhere with a bullet in that empty space between those big ears of yours."

"Wow. You really do care. Have you told Deb how you feel?"

"That's enough of that. Have you seen Jones?"

"Not since I left the office. What's up?"

"We need to meet. I have a lot to tell you which you just may not believe."

"All right. I'll be at your house in about an hour."

"I'm not at the house."

"Didn't I tell you to stay there? Now who's the one with the bad air between the ears?"

"When I couldn't get hold of you, I went looking for you. I went to your apartment and found Bubba gone too; that put up more red flags than you'd find in China. Simmons told me about the GPS blocker he gave you and we had no way to locate you then. You should have kept me informed."

"Sam, you're on suspension and I didn't want to get you into any more trouble. I've been busy and I think I have a way to make things right. Do you remember the first place we ever had lunch together?"

"No."

"Great. I forgot how short everything was on you,

including your memory. How about where I caused you to spill coffee on yourself."

"Now that, I remember."

"Can you meet me there in half an hour? Make sure you're not followed."

"I'm sorry, who's this again?"

"Sam!"

"Okay, okay. Half an hour it is."

Gillam got to the fast food restaurant first and backed into a parking space. He saw Sam pull in a few minutes later. He kept an eye on everything and it didn't look like there had been anyone tailing him. Sam parked and went over to Larry's vehicle and got in on the passenger side. He looked at his friend for a few seconds before speaking.

"I made a check of my car before coming and didn't find any bugs or GPS units. I made a lot of turns and stops and didn't see anyone following me. I think we're Okay."

"Good. Same here. Now tell me what's going on."

"Where's Bubba?"

"I've got him stashed away at a hotel. I didn't think he was going to be safe at my apartment anymore. I've got a lot to tell you as well."

After Lovett got through explaining the conversations he had had with Agent McGill and Doctor Higdon, Gillam just shook his head.

"It's bigger than I thought," he finally said. "Does anyone know how Jones got involved with this mess? Not like it really matters now."

"No. There might be some speculation. Better yet, what are we going to do about all this other stuff now? What plan has come from that mighty brain?"

"Well, if you must know." And then he told Sam what he had been doing since he watched him drive away. He told him the plan, which had come about by necessity. For survivals sake. And how he had started it in motion.

"And the judge went along with this?" Sam was impressed. "You've got big ones, bud. Huge."

"Are you ready to back me up on this?"

"I'll always be there for you partner. I'm locked and loaded, but I don't have a badge or ID. I have no police power right now, but who gives a flying fig tree. I wouldn't miss it. I only wish I could be the one to do it."

Jenny had gone to her room complaining of being ill. She said she was stopped up, dizzy and had a massive headache. It had been one of the very few times she had apparently caught something while at The Facility.

She made sure everyone knew she was sick and apparently getting sicker. She wanted people to avoid her in caution of coming down with whatever she had. She even put a sign on the outside of her door saying she was sick and please not to disturb her.

She told Mrs. Pettigrew she would be fine for duty in a day or so after receiving some medication from the infirmary, but right now, she needed to rest. Mrs. Pettigrew agreed with her. She knew Jenny was not a malingerer and this was one of the few times she missed any work. No need to spread anything around and have too many others come down with something to slow down the assignments. Just give her a couple days to get over it. All for the best.

William N. Gilmore

CHAPTER 37

King woke with a start. It was still dark outside. Someone was in the room with him. He reached over and turned on the lamp next to the bed. A figure was sitting in a chair facing him. The figure held a semi-automatic with a silencer on it. King started to go for the nightstand drawer.

"Don't bother," said the figure. King turned back to the man. His eyes were still adjusting to the light and the figure was slowly becoming recognizable.

The man was patting a gun, his gun, on the chairs arm.

"Didn't want you to have an accident in your sleep."

"Richards!" King was finally able to see. "What are you doing?"

"Being loyal. More than you can say. The general is very disappointed in you, captain. So am I. Seems you just can't keep your mouth shut. Talking to people you shouldn't. We can't have that. Get dressed."

"Where are we going? To see the general?"

"I said, get dressed. Unless you want it right here?" He pointed the gun at him. "Doesn't matter to me. I just didn't want to carry dead weight." He smiled at his own joke. "Get it."

King got slowly out of bed. The gun followed his every move. No chance to make any kind of attack on Richards. He knew he would be dead before he hit the floor. He would have to wait and he knew Richards would be expecting it. He got dressed in clothes from the night before. No shower or shave. He didn't even let him brush his teeth. He grabbed his wallet, his keys and his watch. Richards had him leave his cell phone and toss the keys over to him.

"Now we're going out to your car. Anything funny and you won't see the sunrise. Clear?" The man tucked the other gun away in the small of his back.

"Yes." All the time, King's mind was racing. Looking for an escape. A plan. As long as he was breathing, there was a chance.

They went the short distance to King's car, parked in the BOQ parking lot. There was no one around. Not even the early morning joggers were out to see Richards pointing a gun at King's back, directing him to the passenger side of a car.

"Get in and scoot over, keeping your hands in sight."

After King complied, he was told to fasten his seatbelt.

"For safety's sake, you know. Don't want you getting stopped by any nasty police, now do we?" He then got in and closed the door. The whole time keeping the gun on King. He opened the glove box and made sure there were no hidden weapons there.

"Drive out the main gate and get onto Lee Street," he said, handing him the keys. "Head towards town. I'll give you directions then."

"We're not going to The Facility?"

"You go where I tell you to go. Now drive. Both hands on the wheel. Don't speed, don't swerve, and watch that brake. With one hand, not taking the gun off King, Richards also put on his seatbelt.

Took care of that idea, King thought.

He drove out the main gate of Ft. McPherson, got out on Lee Street, and headed towards downtown, just as he had been told. There was no traffic to speak of. The streetlights had a weird bluish glow and all the traffic lights were flashing amber for blocks down the street.

He drove parallel to railroad tracks that had railcars sitting on one set of tracks and he could hear the whistle of a train which must have been coming through on another. Up ahead on his right, he saw a set of railroad crossing guards come down, blocking one of the side streets that crossed over the tracks. The train was near. He looked in the rearview mirror and he could see the light of the train coming from behind.

King made some quick calculations. Richards was turned more towards King than straight ahead. He was keeping one eye on the road ahead and one eye on King. The automatic was being held in such a way that it was aimed right at King's side.

With the addition of the silencer, the barrel was about ten-inches long and made the gun front-heavy. Richards had his gun hand resting on his right leg for support. King made his assessment and knew what he had to do. There was another side street which crossed the tracks only about two blocks away now.

This might be his only chance. There was no guarantee this would work. His timing had to be near perfect or whatever he did wouldn't matter. He'd probably be dead either way. This was going to be crazy.

There were lines of blues and pinks and grays just above the horizon to the East as Azira gathered with his people at the garage. Some were rubbing their eyes after a long night of preparation and some from just waking up. Things were about to become interesting.

Azira had had the two guys who were going to Black Bird Distributors do numerous dry runs with the equipment to make sure everything worked right and ran smooth. He also wanted to make sure they knew the risks, just in case they were discovered, and what their cover story was going to be.

They went over several different scenarios with different obstacles and problems. Of course, you couldn't plan for every little thing and once they were inside, out of contact, anything could happen.

There would be no more contact with Jenny so everything had to happen as she was expecting. There could be no changes. And with that said, she also couldn't contact The Magician if she had had any problems herself.

A lot could happen with plans chiseled in a single piece of stone. As with the plan, just like that worked piece of stone,

one misstep could destroy all the hard work and there was no starting over. Lives were in the balance.

Larry had been thankful Sam had taken care of Cali until he could get back to the apartment. After he had gotten home and settled in, he called Connie and they talked for a while. He didn't go into any details about Sam's and his plans for the next day.

They talked about what each other liked or disliked, their favorite things, places they wanted to go, hopes and dreams. It relaxed him and took all the troubles away for a while. He hoped he wasn't being too childish.

Reality hit the next morning. He had just gotten out of the shower and was getting dressed when his new cell phone rang. It had no caller ID on it, but he knew it was Sam. They arranged to meet at the hotel baring any complications.

Larry packed a bag with clean clothes for Bubba along with toilet articles. If he was going to be with him, he didn't want to have to worry about his hygiene. He would get there plenty of time ahead of Sam to get Bubba cleaned and dressed and have him ready to roll when he got there. It was going to be an interesting day for everyone.

William N. Gilmore

CHAPTER 38

King wanted to get the timing just right. He slowed the car just a little, but it was enough for Richards to notice.

"What are you doing? Get a move on."

"You don't want me speeding, do you? I thought you didn't want me to get stopped by the police."

"That's right, but you won't if you're doing the speed limit, which you aren't. Speed up."

"But there's a cop on my tail."

Richards took a quick glance to the rear and that's all King needed to make his move. Just as they came upon one of the side streets, he jerked the steering wheel all the way to the right, going up a slight incline of the adjoining street, causing Richards to suddenly lean way over towards him. The gun was now in front of King's chest.

He grabbed the silencer just as Richards pulled the trigger. The bullet shattered the driver's side window, sending glass all over King. King forced the gun up and back, breaking the hold Richards had on it. The car continued up the street's incline towards the railroad tracks and struck the metal crossing barrier, causing the car to careen to the left, but still on an angle towards the tracks and now, the on-coming train.

Richards tried to grab the gun back and at the same time,

245

using his left arm, put King into a headlock. Richards couldn't quite get far enough to get his arm in position due to his seatbelt.

King and Richards both had hold of the gun now, but King used his right elbow and smashed Richards in the face several times. Richards would not let go of the gun and with his left hand now free, went for the one in the small of his back.

He brought it around as he was about to be hit again, and just as the car and the train collided. It caught the right front of the car, crushing it instantly, gripping it as if it were in a vice and pushed it down the track.

The squeals of metal against metal were almost deafening. Sparks and pieces of metal flew everywhere. The tires exploded. The cars one remaining headlight, danced its light along the rails and gravel under the car, then went dead.

The startled train engineer had seen the car coming towards the track, but thought for sure it would have stopped. Even after it hit the barricade, he thought it would somehow stop before it got to the track. He applied the brake and watched in horror, unable to do anything else.

The train continued to push the crushed piece of metal down the track for another fifty yards or so until it finally came to rest. Smoke came from the car and the engineer thought it would burst into flames at any time. He didn't know if anyone had survived the crash or if they could. He jumped down from the engine and ran to the car carrying a flashlight and a fire extinguisher.

The front and right side of the car were demolished. He ran around to the open door of the driver's side. When he looked in, he was sickened by what he saw. Then he was mystified. The person in the passenger seat, still wearing a seatbelt, had been pretty much mangled and squashed into pulp. All except a left arm and hand.

The hand held a gun. It looked like an automatic. In the flashlight's beam, he wasn't sure, but it looked like the finger on the trigger was twitching a little.

He looked around thinking he would see the driver on the ground somewhere. Not finding anyone, he was afraid they might be under the car or possibly the train. Hearing sirens in the distance, he thought he would let the police or the fire department find that one. He'd seen enough.

The soft cover over the city which had been the night, was beginning to lighten and spread to become the day. The black was turning a soft purple and pink.

The blue and red lights of the police cars, fire trucks, and ambulances flooded the crash scene and mixed with nearby traffic lights as they changed over to their regular duty of reds, yellows, and greens. It was a light show any kid would love and one which would make most grown-ups cringe. No one noticed the figure several hundred feet away, holding his right side, limping away along the road by the railroad tracks.

William N. Gilmore

CHAPTER 39

Azira and his teams were on the move. They wanted to be in position before the truck reached the gate. This was it. No turning back now.

Jenny was up and ready. She had packed a small fanny pack with her stuff. Now she only had to wait. Just like she had been doing all night long.

Gillam had Bubba ready when Sam arrived at the hotel. Bubba was very nervous. Both detectives tried to assure him he would be in no danger and they would be with him the whole time. He would ride with Gillam and Sam would follow until they got to their destination and set up. Then all Bubba had to do was give the pre-arranged signal and let the detectives do the rest. Gillam went over the signal several times with Bubba so there would be no mistakes. Then he decided to go over it with him several more times.

Lieutenant Jones was in the shower letting cold water soak his head. The hangover wasn't as bad as most. The hooker he had just kicked out wasn't as bad as most either. He had wanted to celebrate a little early. This was the day which should rid him of most of his problems.

He would get the judge to sign the warrants for Gillam and Lovett this morning and then in the pretense of trying to make an arrest, he would set them up and knock them down.

He would call them up, have them meet him, explaining that Lovett had been cleared. He could have his gun and badge back and get back on the job. Before they knew what hit them, they would have neat, little, round holes in their big, ugly, round heads.

The pain he got from his little laugh was worth it to him. He was sure he would be laughing a lot more later.

As Azira sat in a car some distance away, he watched the lift truck as it approached the guardhouse of Black Bird Distributors. The sun had just peaked over some of the buildings and gave a blinding glare. He squinted to see what was happening through the binoculars.

The guard handed the driver a clipboard and pen and received them back just a few seconds later. The guard, using the pen was pointing to one of the large roll-up doors and then stepped back as the truck moved forward.

"So far so good," he said.

The truck drove over to the door and then backed it in, leaving room for the lift to operate. The passenger got out, ran over to the main walk-through door, and pressed the button on the intercom. The passenger disappeared inside the building.

After a short wait, Azira could see the roll-up door opening. At its entrance were the truck's passenger and his warehouse escort. It was the same man who had escorted him to the bathroom. Good thing he wasn't with the truck after all.

The driver of the truck adjusted the lift so it was even with the loading dock and there was no space under it. A pretty good job, Azira thought.

The driver and passenger undid the straps on the soda machine on the back of the truck. It was already on a large dolly. That made it much easier to move.

Just then, Azira watched as another car approached the guardhouse. It was a taxi. The guard saw the passenger, gave a sloppy salute and waved it on. It drove over to the front entrance where it dropped off its passenger before heading back out. The man, dressed in rumpled clothing and — was he missing a shoe? —went up to the door and using an electronic key card, opened it. He did this with his left hand. He never took his hand off his right side. Strange, Azira thought.

When Azira looked back over at the roll-up door, he saw it had been lowered. Everyone was inside the warehouse now. He hoped he would see them again, soon.

Jenny rubbed her eyes for a bit and put a little water on her face before she left her room and went to Mrs. Pettigrew's office. She knocked on the door and Mrs. Pettigrew told her to come in.

"Mrs. Pettigrew, I still feel really bad. I'm going to the infirmary this morning and then back to bed if that's all right with you."

"Of course, dear. You look terrible. I'll make sure you're not disturbed, but I will need you tomorrow. We can't let things get too far behind."

"Oh, yes. I'm sure I'll be fine by tomorrow. I just need the rest to get better."

The man escorted the workers/rescuers with the machine around several corridors to get to the break room where the broken machine was located. When they got there, they looked at the machine and one of the men hit his forehead with the palm of his hand.

"I forgot my tool box. It's back at the truck. Can you take me back there?" He asked the man.

The escort looked at the two men and then told the one. "You stay here with the machine. Don't go anywhere. We'll be right back."

"Okay, I'll just get it ready," he said, as he began to undo the straps.

As the man escorted the worker back through the corridors, they passed a young lady.

"Good morning, Ms. Jordan. How are you today?"

"I'm not very well right now, so I'm going to be in my

room all day."

"I'm sorry to hear that. Good news though. They're here
to replace the broken soda machine in the break room. I
understand you had a problem with it."

"Yes, that is good news. Thank you."

Jenny hurried to the break room. No one else was there,
but the worker who had taken all the straps off and was standing
by.

"Are you Jenny, the *Wonder Woman?*"

"Oh, yes, thank you. Are you The Magician?" She asked
hoping to finally meet.

"Me?" He laughed a little. "No. He's close though. We
don't have much time. We have to hurry."

He used a special key and began to get the door to the
soda machine open. When he had it open, the insides were not
the insides of a soda machine. There was a jump seat like the
ones airline attendants would sit in for takeoffs and landings. A
motorcycle helmet was strapped to it. There was also padding all
around as well as handles for her to hold on to for stabilization.
The trip out might be a little shaky.

"Put on the helmet and strap yourself in with the seatbelt
and shoulder harness. We hope you enjoy your ride on Freedom
Airways."

Just as she began to get into the machine, Captain King
came around the corner.

William N. Gilmore

CHAPTER 40

Gillam and Lovett parked their cars on the side of Pryor Street, at the parking meters. Although parking wasn't permitted until 9 a.m., there were still a few cars there. Mostly sheriff's cars and a few off-duty cops headed for court. The morning traffic was already heavy as it usually was in that area.

Gillam had Bubba sit on a nearby bench under a shady poplar tree. He gave him the hat he had bought. Of course, it was too small. Now he wished he had bought the wig. Not for the disguise effect, but just because it would make Bubba look even sillier. That was cruel. He should give Bubba a break. Nah, not this week.

Sam took up a position across the street. There was a guy drawing a small crowd with foreclosure auctions about to happen on the steps of the courthouse. Sam blended in.

Larry went into the courthouse and was watching through the glass doors. He had an eye on Bubba and Sam, as well as the street. This would be the only entrance open now.

Jones arrived just a few minutes later and also parked his white Toyota Avalon on Pryor Street. He exited his car and began to cross the street.

Bubba gave the signal they were looking for. He took off the hat and waved it a few times. He also began pointing at

Jones. Not part of the signal. Bubba had no problem recognizing Jones as the murderer of Kim. The signal was just a confirmation.

Jones began up the steps of the courthouse just as Gillam exited the door. Jones looked up startled and stopped in his tracks.

"What are you doing here, Gillam? I thought you were taking a few days off with your little butt buddy, Lovett."

"I could ask you the same thing, lieutenant."

"I have an appointment with a judge, but that's none of your business."

"Oh, it might be. It wouldn't be with Judge Freeman, now, would it?"

"I think you need to get out of my way, sergeant. That's an order."

"Bite my butt, lieutenant. And that's not a request. Judge Freeman has removed herself from office. She's no longer under your thumb."

"What are you talking about," he muttered. His eyes narrowing at Gillam.

"Lieutenant Mark Jones, I have warrants for your arrest for the murder of George Kim, attempted murder, arson, and a crap load of other charges."

"Doesn't that just suck?" Jones heard come from behind him. He turned and saw Lovett near the bottom of the steps. He was wearing a big smile and holding an even bigger gun.

"Your weapon if you please, lieutenant," Gillam requested, holding out his left hand. "Nice and slow."

Just at that time there was a loud yell, 'Gun!', from somewhere near them. The next thing Gillam knew, Sam was being tackled by a big uniformed guy. Jones grabbed Gillam's hand, yanking him down the steps of the courthouse, causing him to tumble down to the sidewalk. Jones took off, running across the street.

Bubba saw everything on the steps happen at once and then saw Jones running across the street. He thought he might be running for him. Bubba began to run in the other direction as fast as his little fat legs could carry him.

Jones didn't pay any attention to the big guy. He was running for his car. He pulled the keys out, hitting the unlock button on the remote and got to the car just as Gillam was getting up. Gillam was about to run after Jones, but Lovett had a big Sheriff's Deputy on top of him, ready to cuff him.

"He's my partner" he yelled at the Sheriff, showing him his badge. Pointing towards Jones, he said, "That's the bad guy."

Jones had made it to his car and was getting in as Gillam ran out into the street, gun drawn. Jones took off, squealing tires, almost running Gillam over just before he jumped out of the way.

Gillam picked himself up again. He ran to his car, jumped in and started after Jones. It was not what they had planned. Not knowing whom to trust and not wanting any word going out, they didn't call for, nor expect a need for any back up except each other.

There may also have been a little ego boosting as well as revenge going on there. All that was over now. Jones was on the run. He was being pursued and had nothing to lose. He was armed and more than a little desperate. They needed to get him before he hurt someone or got away.

Sam, having been released by the deputy, ran to his car as well. Bubba was there about to get in on the passenger side.

"Oh no, big guy. I don't have the room and I don't have the horsepower to drag you along right now. Sorry."

Bubba stood there despondent as Sam took off, trying desperately to catch up.

CHAPTER 41

The rescuer's eyes almost bugged out. Jenny froze. King was holding a large gun in his left hand. It had what looked like a silencer on it. His right hand didn't quite cover a large, wet, red spot on his right side.

"What are you doing, Ms. Jordan?"

Jenny couldn't speak. Her eyes darted from the gun, to the wound, and back again. The counterfeit soda company worker quickly put his hands up.

"Put your hands down." The young man did. Slowly. "What's going on here?" King asked, again.

"Please," was all Jenny could get out right then.

"Trying to get out of here with a little help from some friends? I don't blame you too much, Ms. Jordan."

"I'm being kept prisoner here. I have family, friends. I wanted to go back to school. I have a life. Would you want to be kept here against your will?"

"Oh, but I am, Ms. Jordan. Not like you of course, but believe me, I am a prisoner to everything that's going on here. And there's no escape for me." He winced and gave a grunt, bending slightly, but not lowering the gun pointed at them.

"You're hurt. What happened? Can I help?" Jenny took a step towards King.

"Don't worry about it," he said, taking a step back. "You think that even if you got out of here, General Cunningham would let you stay out? Don't you think he would come after you? You know too much."

"But I've got to try," Jenny pleaded. "I don't belong here."

The other fake worker/rescuer had stalled his escort as long as he could and they returned to the break room just then. They walked over to the others beside the open soda machine. That's when the escort saw the gun, the blood, and the reconfigured insides of the soda machine.

"What's going on here, Captain King? What is this?"

Gillam was quickly catching up to Jones. They had turned onto Trinity Street and made a quick left onto Central Avenue, but now, Jones' progress was stalled by heavy traffic. He wasn't going to let a few cars and some traffic lights get in his way. He went around a line of cars stopped at a red light, driving up on the sidewalk, causing people to scurry for cover and safety.

He ran the red light causing other cars coming down Martin Luther King Boulevard to hit their brakes, resulting in at least one rear end collision. It made Gillam's going a little easier with the traffic already stopped.

Sam was still at least a block behind and falling back quickly. His little four-cylinder car just didn't have the get-up-

and-go Gillam's had, nor did he have the driving expertise, or the inclination to slam it into someone. He tried Larry's cell. No answer.

Both Jones and Gillam dodged cars and pedestrians as they sped through the morning parade of commuters on their way to the daily grind of boring jobs, too long meetings, and even more boring lectures at the area schools. Many blew their horns. Some gave them the one finger salute.

Jones continued up Central until he made a wide turn onto Edgewood Avenue. He almost hit a Ford truck head-on, sideswiping it with the left front of his Avalon, but managing to regain control of his car just before hitting a parked one. Jones never stopped and barely slowed. Gillam kept right with him.

Gillam knew that Jones was still armed and didn't want to get too close just yet. He was sure Jones would take some shots if he got the chance. As bad as he wanted to get Jones, he didn't want any innocent citizens hurt by stray bullets or out of control cars. He had it in his mind though that he was not about to let Jones get away.

They passed under I-75 and then passed the Dr. Martin Luther King tomb on their left. Gillam was only about thirty yards behind Jones. He hoped Jones would crash into some solid object, get several flats, or maybe even run out of gas. He wasn't real sure where he was running. Where could he go? His career was over. He would most likely spend the rest of his life in jail, if not worse. But he had to catch him first.

The second worker/rescuer put his hands up after seeing the gun. He thought for sure everything was over. Including his life.

"Put your hands down," King told him. He did, very slowly.

King looked at the escort for a second then raised his gun slightly. The gun made a louder than expected report, even with the silencer attached. It wasn't like in the movies. The escort dropped to the floor with a hole between his eyes. Both rescuers simultaneously put their hands up. Jenny's mouth opened as if to scream, but nothing came out.

"Put your hands down," he told the young men again. They did. Very quickly. King went over to the escort and with a grimace, bent over and took the dead man's ID badge which also opened the controlled access doors. He handed it to Jenny.

"Get out of here, Ms. Jordan. Go live your life. Get married, have lots of babies. Don't ever talk about this place. Don't worry about the general. I'm about to take care of that problem for both of us."

"What about you?" Jenny asked. "What are you going to do?" She looked at his side with real concern.

He removed his blood-covered hand from his wound. There was a large hole in his side and blood was oozing out. The wet blood spot had become the size of a medium pizza and had traveled down his pants to his one shoe. If he didn't get medical attention soon, he most likely would bleed out.

"I don't think I have much choice. I might have enough time to give you a head start before all Hell breaks loose here." He pointed to the soda machine with the barrel of the gun. "Get in there. Don't let all their hard work go to waste. Get out of here. Now!"

Jones made another quick turn, tires yelling out from the torture they were under. He skidded to a stop on Randolph Street and waited for Gillam to make the turn. As soon as he saw him, he fired out the driver's side window.

The first shot hit the windshield on the passenger side. Gillam ducked down at the same time he hit the brake, turning the steering wheel to the left. Several shots hit the right side of Gillam's Santa Fe. One took out the passenger side window.

As Larry came to a stop, he rose, taking a quick peek, dropping back down in a hurry. Jones was already starting to drive off. No chance for Gillam to take his own shot. He got up and started after Jones again.

William N. Gilmore

CHAPTER 42

Sam had lost the two cars. He had a pretty good idea which way they headed. He didn't have a radio and Larry wasn't answering his cell. He didn't see any patrol cars around. He would just have to keep searching and maybe get lucky. He hoped Larry was having luck as well.

King took off as Jenny put on the helmet and got into the soda machine. She strapped herself in and braced herself as the workers closed and secured the machine's door. A small light came on inside so she was not in total darkness. A small bit of comfort they had thought about.

She could feel the machine being jostled around a bit and then tilted back on the dolly. She was sitting at an angle now, with her head back. With the helmet on and all the padding, she felt like an astronaut about to take off. In fact, as they started to move, that's exactly what she imagined.

She closed her eyes and thought of heading to the stars and planets. She was passing Mars and headed towards Jupiter with its big red spot. The spot grew until it turned into King's bloody wound. She quickly opened her eyes. Her thoughts now changed. She wondered why King had let her go. How had he gotten the wound? What were his plans for General

Cunningham? Was she really about to be free?

Jones wasn't giving up. Not without a fight. Or rather, a shootout. He continued driving like a wild man. He made a right on Highland Avenue and punched it. His speed got up to around forty miles an hour. About the best he could do in the traffic. Gillam was able to stay with him, but not too close.

Gillam checked and had plenty of gas, but saw his temperature gauge was going way over to the hot side. It was possible one of Jones' shots had done some damage. He was going to need to end this soon.

Jones crossed over Boulevard and was headed up towards the Jimmy Carter Presidential Library. There was a lot of traffic around that area in the mornings. The area was also swarming with bicycles and joggers. There were several streets he could choose which would take him to almost any corner of the city.

Larry noticed his car was starting to smoke, or was that steam. He didn't smell smoke. It had to be the hot water from a damaged radiator or pipe. It wouldn't be long and he would be out of the chase. Jones might get away.

Jones took one more turn. He got onto Freedom Parkway right at the Carter Library. He headed back in the other direction. Gillam knew he only had a few minutes left to do something. He gave his engine all he could, hoping it would last.

Jones was going full tilt now and was doing about fifty when he came upon stopped traffic where it crossed Boulevard.

He slowed and tried to go around several cars and get through the intersection on a red light. He didn't make it. A van hit the left rear of his car, turning it completely around before he struck a light pole on the far side of the intersection.

Gillam slowed, ready to stop and jump out and rush the car, gun drawn. He didn't get the chance. Somehow, Jones' car was still moving. He spun the wheels, throwing up gravel, and took off. The right front wheel was wobbly at best and the left rear tire was flat; the wheels appeared about to drop off.

Gillam couldn't believe it. Jones was still trying to get away in his car, but it was only doing about twenty miles an hour. With the extensive damage, that was probably the best it could do. Gillam got across the intersection and continued after Jones. He was headed down Freedom Parkway towards I-75 Southbound. The large bridge complex looping over I-75 had a big curved ramp going down to the freeway. Towards the end of the ramp, on the right-hand side of the concrete barricades, were the flat tops of buildings which looked like they would be close enough to touch.

Just as Jones was getting to the bottom of the ramp, Gillam caught up and rammed him, sending the Toyota into the barricades. Both cars were done. All the traffic on the bridge had stopped. People sitting in their cars were awe struck while watching the incident play out without getting too close.

Steam, and now smoke came from Gillam's car. The airbag had startled him for a moment giving Jones time to get out of his car and begin running down the ramp. Jones had his gun out and fired several rounds over his shoulder at Gillam as he ran. The shots were wide and Gillam, with his own gun drawn yelled several times for Jones to stop.

"Throw your gun down, lieutenant. Stop where you are." He fired one shot which hit the street next to Jones. Jones stopped and turned. He was about twenty yards from Gillam. Jones raised his weapon and took aim. Gillam already had a bead on him. Both fired at the same time.

The hopeful rescuers got back to the roll-up doors with the occupied soda machine. They got it open and Azira could see them as they loaded the machine onto the truck. There was no signal that all had gone well as they had been instructed to give. The escort did not appear to be with them. The workers hurriedly strapped the machine onto the bed and got into their truck.

Ms. Pettigrew wanted to see if the new soda machine had been delivered as promised and try it out herself before the new shift came in. As she went to the break room, she noticed someone had dripped what appeared to be red paint on the floor.

There were drops almost every few inches. She would call maintenance and let them know. Sloppy people, she thought. She tried to remember what might have been on schedule to be painted and couldn't come up with anything.

When she got to the break room, instead of finding a new

machine, she found one of her co-workers on the floor. He may have slipped on some of the paint that was on the floor and hit his head.

As she turned him over, she saw a lot more paint on the linoleum, she also saw the small round hole in his head. The realization hit her with full force. She screamed as she ran back towards her office, yelling for security instead of maintenance.

The truck was just beginning to exit the gate when a loud horn started blowing at the warehouse. The guard looked towards the warehouse where the alarm horn sounded and then back at the truck.

Startled at the realization the truck was the reason for the alarm, he ran after it, trying to stop the truck, but it was already too late. The truck with its precious cargo sped out and away.

William N. Gilmore

CHAPTER 43

Jones was hit in his right shoulder. He fell backwards, dropping his weapon. Gillam was struck in his left leg; no bone, just meat. It hurt like the dickens, but it wasn't life threatening.

"Show me your hands, lieutenant," Gillam shouted. The gun had fallen several feet away from Jones. Jones clutched his injured shoulder and got up on one knee.

"It's over, Jones." Gillam said, not giving him the respect of the title any longer. Gillam limped towards him, his gun at his side.

"Not yet. Not just yet." Jones got up and began running towards the right-side barricades. He pulled his personal weapon from the small of his back and began firing at Gillam. Gillam opened up on him as well. As Jones got to the barricades, he tried to make a leap for the roof of a building. Gillam saw him disappear.

Gillam ran the best he could over to the barricade and did a quick look over. The roof of the building, which appeared as if it were right there, was nearly twenty feet away. It had been an optical illusion. Looking closer than it truly was.

He looked down. Under the bridge was a parking lot which had a wrought iron security fence surrounding it. Along the top of the fence, the top posts had spikes every eight inches or so.

The back of Jones' head had caught one of the spikes and stopped; his body didn't. Jones had dropped about thirty-seven feet from the bridge to the parking lot. The rest of him, only thirty.

Larry tried to call Sam on his cell; it was dead as well. He had forgotten to charge it.

The truck pulled into a pre-designated area to meet with Azira. As the driver got out, Azira wanted to know what happened. Why was there no signal?

"We got her," the driver said, his voice shaky at best. "But there were some problems." They got up on the back of the truck and started releasing the straps. With his unsteady hands, it took the driver several times to get the key inserted. Finally, the driver began to open the fake soda machine door.

"As long as you have her out safe, that's all that matters."

"There's a dead guy back there. We didn't do it. Some other guy shot him and then let us leave."

"Okay, we'll talk about it later. Let's get her out."

The door to the soda machine opened wide. Inside was a figure. An obviously female figure. That was easy to tell even with her wearing the helmet.

The seat straps were loosened and Jenny stepped out a little wobbly. Azira grabbed her arm to steady her. She took off the helmet and shook her head. Even though there had been a light in the machine, her eyes were not accustomed to the bright sunshine. The months of artificial light affected her eyes and she had to squint and hold her hand up to block the light. There was a face slowly coming into focus. She could tell it was smiling.

"Hi. I'm Azira Hazar. I'm The Magician. Welcome back to the real world."

Jenny grabbed him, throwing her arms around his neck. "Thank you. Thank you, so much." She buried her face in his chest and couldn't stop crying.

"You're safe now," he said, hesitating a second before putting his arms around her, a few tears at his eyes as well. The rest of the group around them started clapping and cheering. Some fairytales do come true.

William N. Gilmore

CHAPTER 44

King knew he didn't have long. Not the way he was bleeding, and now that the alarm had been triggered. Someone must have discovered the body.

He made his way through the corridors and was headed for the general's office. He hoped he was there. He grimaced as he climbed a set of stairs to the next level. Just as he was about to take the last step to the landing, a security guard opened the access door.

"Captain King. What's going on?"

"There's an intruder on the level below! He shot me!"

The security guard started down the steps with his gun drawn. When he passed by King, King shot him in the head. The guard tumbled down the steps, coming to rest at an awkward angle. He was going to get the security guards gun, but it had fallen even further down the steps. He wasn't sure he could make the trip there and back up the steps.

He went through the door on that level after making sure everything was clear. He went down several corridors until he came to the section he wanted. He went in. There was no one in the outer office so he showed himself into the general's. The man himself was sitting behind the large desk, smoking one of those god-awful cigars.

"Come in, captain. I thought it might be you coming to visit after I heard about Richards. That looks painful," he said pointing at King's side with the cigar. "Does it hurt?"

King shuffled over to one of the big chairs in front of the desk.

"Not too much," he lied, lowering himself into the chair carefully.

"I could have someone come look at that if you want."

I believe it's a little too late for that, don't you think, general?"

"Maybe so. I was disappointed you went outside my authority with any problems you had. I always thought you would be the one."

"The one what, general?"

"The one that went all the way. Promotions, career. The full military spectrum."

"General, what you're doing here doesn't have anything to do with the military. It's doesn't even have anything to do with the government. It's you. You may have all these people fooled, but not me. I know this is all you. It's your operation, your plan, your misguided attempt to get the country back on track. You think by killing certain people, other people will act the way you want them to. It doesn't work that way. It never has."

The general shook his head. "You're too young to remember about Korea, Viet Nam, Uganda, and many more places like them. With the right incentive, you can get anyone to do anything. You just have to get them to want to do it. At least, more than dying."

"But should you? You're taking away basic human freedom." King was beginning to shake. The blood loss was about to send him into shock.

"Son, don't ever talk to me about freedom. It's freedom I live for and freedom I would die for. Those fools up in Washington don't know squat. They sit in their big fat taxpayer paid-for chairs behind their ornate, protective desks and send young men like you to go fight and die in wars that they make up so they can say that they are looking out for them and the country. Now go out, vote, and get me re-elected. There's the freedom you're thinking about."

"General, you're wrong. You're wrong in your thinking. You're wrong in your actions, and you're wrong believing you can fix it yourself; in this ghoulish way." King began coughing.

He wiped his mouth with the hand which held the gun. Looking at the back of his hand, he saw the bright blood on it. He was so tired. He wanted to shut his eyes and just go to sleep. Not yet, not just yet.

"I may not fix it," the general hissed, "but I might get someone's attention. I'm not alone on this either. There are many like me."

"That's the scary part. Who would be taking your place?"

"And what makes you think I'm going anywhere?"

King held up the gun. He couldn't hold it steady. "I'll make you a deal, general." his voice started to slur. "You quit, you live. Sound good?"

"It looks like all I have to do is just wait a little while. You don't look so good, son."

"And that's another thing. Don't call me son. My dad, although he's gone, is still my real hero." His voice was trailing off. "I would like to think that right now, he's proud of me. Right now ...," King's head started to droop and he jerked it back up.

"Why don't you let me call for a doctor?" The general came from around the back of his desk and sat on the front of it. "Patch you up and then we can talk some more."

King's head dipped again. His chin, all the way to his chest. His eyes, closed.

The general shook his head again. "Poor S.O.B." He walked over to the chair and started to take the gun out of the limp hand. The head didn't rise back up this time, but the hand with the gun did. The silencer wasn't working too well anymore as the two quick shots echoed in the office. With the alarm going off down the corridor, it most likely wasn't heard anyway.

CHAPTER 45

Simmons called Lovett and told him about several 911 calls dealing with gunshots and auto crashes on I-75 at Freedom Parkway, as well as the report of a body on a fence at an Auburn Avenue parking lot not far from that location.

Sam decided to go first to the Freedom Parkway call and found Gillam being treated on the outside of an ambulance for the gunshot wound. He saw the mangled mess of the two cars as well as the gunshot holes in Gillam's Santa Fe.

"Are you okay, Larry?" Sam asked.

"Hell, no! I got shot. What do you think? I fell skateboarding?"

"Well, it looks like you're going to pull through." Sam said, as Larry was looking on the inside of the ambulance.

"He's not there. He won't need a fast ambulance."

"Is he the person on the fence?"

"Yep. It's time to go see him."

After Gillam was treated and bandaged, he signed the release for transport with the ambulance company. He had the uniform officer on the scene make sure no one touched anything inside Jones' car. After the scene was processed, he wanted both cars taken to the impound lot. His poor, crumpled, shot-up Santa Fe was now evidence.

He went over and gingerly got into the passenger side of Sam's little car. He had to put the seat all the way back. Although the wound was considered minor, his leg was still on fire and being cramped didn't help.

Sam drove them down to Auburn Avenue where there was quite a crowd gathering. Many had their cell phone cameras up and snapping pictures. A blanket had been put over the head as well as one over the body until the M.E. arrived. The first officer on the scene recovered a 9mm semi-automatic in the parking lot. It had been placed in a large evidence envelope. He handed it over to Lovett.

"It's got several Teflon coated bullets still in the magazine," Sam discovered. "I bet this is the gun that killed Kim."

"Most likely," Larry stated "We'll get the Crime Lab to do a comparison with the bullet Doctor Higdon has. Sam, I need you to do an inventory of Jones' office. There may be something in there that anyone else would overlook."

"Larry, I'm still on suspension. I don't have any police powers and I don't have the authority to go into the office. Remember?"

"As I recall, you were told you couldn't go back to the office without permission. Well, I'm your superior officer and I'm giving you permission. In fact, that's an order, detective."

"Oh, no. Here we go again."

"And besides, your suspension has been rescinded by

now. Judge Hildebrand arranged to call the chief at 9 a.m. this morning, ordering your reinstatement. More warrants are being handed out for some of Jones' cronies which include Lieutenant Decker and Sergeant Conner. It just so happens we got tied up and missed it."

"Thanks, partner. There's just one more thing I need to do." I just need to see this for myself.

Sam walked over to the fence where a stepladder had been placed to gain access to cover the head with the blanket.

Lifting the blanket, Sam stared into the cold, lifeless eyes of his long-time adversary and said, with a devious grin, "Lieutenant Jones, you've been voted off the planet. Enjoy your time in Hell."

William N. Gilmore

CHAPTER 46

Jenny was taken back to the garage. Everyone wanted to meet her. Everyone wanted to hear what had happened. It still wasn't even clear to her. She was greeted with applause and cheering.

A few in anticipation of a successful rescue had made confetti and streamers. Many wanted a speech, or at least, one from her. She didn't disappoint them. She stood next to Azira on the back of the truck so all could see.

"I just want to say how grateful I am, to everyone. I had no idea there were so many involved in getting me out. I would love to thank each and every one of you personally. Most of all, I want to thank Azira. A true magician. A miracle worker if you will." She grabbed his hand and lifted it high. There were cheers again.

Bubba was still sitting on the bench, under the poplar tree when Gillam and Lovett drove up. How he fit into that car with them, they'll never know. Gillam in the back with his leg up and Bubba spilling over onto Sam as he tried to drive. They took him to the impound lot. His lot.

Doctor Higdon recovered the head and the body of former Atlanta Police Lieutenant Mark Jones. There would be no Atlanta Police Honor Guard; not even a police funeral. He was cremated and his ashes buried without a formal service in a small grave which no one visited and was soon forgotten.

The 9mm recovered by his body was confirmed to be the one used to kill Doctor Kim and the recovered box of Teflon-coated bullets were the same as the one Lovett recovered in the ME's wagon and Jones' car. A red plastic gas can was also recovered from Jones' trunk and the contents proved to be the exact same as the gas in a light bulb which had been intended as a fire bomb.

A search warrant was conducted at Jones' apartment, but nothing more was found to assist in the investigation. It was a strange apartment. There were no televisions or any other electronics located there.

Cocaine and pipes were found in his desk at the Narcotics office which came from crime scenes. His little black book was turned over to the Fulton County District Attorney. A major shakeup in the Atlanta Police Department, as well as several city and county offices was underway.

The next morning, Jenny woke to the sun coming in through the hotel room windows. She had slept in a wonderful soft bed, ate real food, and even got to call her parents; on a secure phone, of course. She didn't tell them everything yet. She wasn't sure if she should. She and Azira had stayed up half the night talking about everything under the sun. He really was cute. She knew she would like him. But things were still in question about her safety and that was foremost on everyone's mind.

Gillam and Lovett met at the office as usual. Gillam still smarted from the gunshot wound, but could get around pretty well. Gillam was notified by the new acting chief that until a new lieutenant was assigned, he was in charge of the Narcotics Squad.

He wanted a search warrant obtained for Black Bird Distributors based upon Jones' connection and the recovery of Cassandra Brown from her back yard. Doctor Higdon had confirmed she had died from the tainted cocaine as well. He put Lovett in charge of writing the search warrant and leading the team.

The warrant was obtained, signed by Judge Hildebrand. The team was assembled, briefed, and they were about to head out. Gillam received a call that changed all that. He had the team stand-down. He had Lovett go with him and they met with Special Agent Tommy McGill just outside the gate of Black Bird Distributors.

"What's going on, Agent McGill?" Gillam asked upon arrival. "Why did you have us cancel?"

"Because there's nothing there." Pointing over to the warehouse. "It's all gone. Striped, cleaned, and dusted. Gone. As if nothing was ever there. I got the go ahead and we did our own raid early this morning."

"What about *Operation Back Street*?" Gillam inquired. "How could it all disappear so quickly? Someone needs to be held accountable."

"I guess you haven't heard any of the news reports this morning?"

"What reports?" The detectives asked, simultaneously.

"There was a military plane crash last night in a remote section of Nevada. Seems there was a Major General Cunningham, his aid, and some civilian contractors that perished in the crash. No survivors, no witnesses, and no bodies. Just ashes. There is no more *Operation Back Street*. In fact, according to official sources, there never was."

"What about the cocaine which was killing everyone who used it," Gillam asked, highly disturbed. Who made it and why? What was in it? We need answers!"

"I don't have any for you," Tommy said, holding his hands out to his sides, empty. "We may never know. Just be glad it's over."

"Are you sure?" Gillam asked.

Tommy couldn't answer that either.

CHAPTER 47

Special Agent Tommy McGill called his friend Azira. He chewed him out, up and down and sideways for disobeying him. He told him what a stupid idea it had been and that he could have gotten himself and others hurt if not worse. It was a wonder how he stayed out of prison.

After letting him swallow that for a while, Tommy also told him he was proud to be his friend. Then he gave him the news on the general and the warehouse. Tommy also made arrangements to drop off a case of iced animal crackers to him as promised. The boy had his weaknesses.

Jenny received the news later that morning from Azira that General Cunningham was dead. *Operation Back Street* was dead too. There were no criminal records on her anywhere, thanks to a certain FBI contact. She was free once more to live her life. There would be no more having to look over her shoulder. She hugged him for what seemed an eternity. He wasn't about to stop her.

That night, John Starling had dinner with a lovely lady; the first of many. Her nephew, beaming the whole evening, was on his best behavior. Curtis gave John a key to the fort. Things were looking good for a change.

Doctor Charles Higdon conducted his own private ceremony with Soo Kim. She was presented with a plaque and a medal, awarded posthumously to her husband, Doctor George Kim, for his duty, above and beyond.

Later, while working in his office, he made a strange discovery. A young man who had been killed in a tragic car-train accident had his fingerprints listed as CLASSIFIED. He had picture identification on him, but it was found to be bogus. This was too much of a coincidence. He was glad he hadn't sent the copies of *The Bomb* back yet.

As of yet, neither he nor the Crime Lab could discover the process by which the cocaine turned into an instant killing machine. He hoped that information had died as well.

Jaccob Mutumbo was shooting hoops behind the ME's Office. He looked up at the twilight sky and seeing a few stars, wondered how the sky looked in a far-away land; a land he missed and hoped to get back to soon, with a knowledge which could help his country.

Sam and Debbie sat outside, holding hands as they gazed at the same night sky. A shooting star crossed the area they were observing. Both said "Wow" at the same time and laughed. Their hands squeezed tighter. Deb rubbed her tummy with the other.

Larry just got off the phone with Connie. This weekend they would get together and walk some trails, putting his leg to work again. They planned to go gold panning in North Georgia, and maybe even go to a ballgame. But then again, maybe not the ballgame.

Larry was still a little restless and had a hard time sleeping. It was hard to relax after so much which had happened recently. There was still a lot on his mind. His leg didn't hurt as bad and he decided to go for a drive in his rented car. It wasn't his Santa Fe, but it was a nice car.

Larry got on some back roads and was enjoying the breeze through the windows and some soft music on the radio. There was no traffic. It was as if he were alone in the world. He was starting to relax a bit now. Drives always did that for him.

The radio suddenly turned to static and he thought he was losing the radio station, but the car began losing power as well, and the headlights were flickering. He made it to a cut-out in the roadway before it came to a stop on its own. He thought he would have to call for a tow truck. Maybe he would call Bubba.

He got his cell phone out. He had charged it this time, but it showed no signal and then went out altogether. The engine on the car died. The lights flickered and then went totally out. Nothing worked on it.

Larry got out of the car. He was surrounded by the dark,

the trees, and the stars. He was being sung to by a variety of nature's creatures. The sky was endless and the stars were so clear in the moonless night.

His neck was starting to strain from looking up so long, but he couldn't stop. The crickets and other night musicians suddenly ceased their serenade, and he thought he heard a slight humming sound. It wasn't the car and there were no other vehicles on the road. It seemed to be more of a vibration than anything. Something he could feel inside himself.

Suddenly, a light appeared in the sky. It was bright and pulsating. It was hard for him to look directly at it. He held up a hand to block the light with an attempt to see past it.

Whatever it might be it was now moving slowly over him. It was impossible to tell how big it was or exactly how far away. A red beam hit him in the eyes, blinding him for a second, causing him to look down. The beam was now on his chest. He felt a sting like the mother of all hornets just got hold of him.

Gilliam's rental car was found by the Georgia State Patrol early that morning, abandoned just off a road about fifty miles from his apartment. The driver's door was open and a cell phone lay on the driver's seat. The keys were still in the ignition. Larry Gillam was nowhere to be found.

To be continued in the
exciting new book

BLUE KNIGHTS

&

WHITE LIES

A Larry Gillam and Sam Lovett Novel

by

William N. Gilmore

Made in the USA
Lexington, KY
29 September 2018